GO HOME, RICKY!

GO HOME, RICKY!

A NOVEL

GENE KWAK

THE OVERLOOK PRESS, NEW YORK

This edition first published in hardcover in 2021 by
The Overlook Press, an imprint of ABRAMS
195 Broadway, 9th floor
New York, NY 10007
www.overlookpress.com

Abrams books are available at special discounts when purchased in quantity
for premiums and promotions as well as fundraising or educational use.
Special editions can also be created to specification. For details,
contact specialsales@abramsbooks.com or the address above.

Library of Congress Control Number: 2021934869

Printed and bound in the United States

1 3 5 7 9 10 8 6 4 2

ISBN: 978-1-4197-5361-9
eISBN: 978-1-64700-255-8

ABRAMS The Art of Books
195 Broadway, New York, NY 10007
abramsbooks.com

For Mom and Dad,
the best tag team duo since Shawn Michaels and Marty Jannetty

Sometimes . . . the whole show gets old, but then we use drugs, and we wreck a lot of fresh flesh and then we wake and feel guilty.

—Barry Hannah

I never saw a wild thing sorry for itself.

—D. H. Lawrence

go home (verb): said by one wrestler to another, meaning to finish the match

CHAPTER ONE

LISTEN TO THOSE blue collars. All slab bellies and seed-and-feed hats. Screaming my name in their gut-deep, cig-scorched voices. Heard a stat that the most prone to playing sad sax solos are ag hands. Farmers. Laborers. Ranchers. If I can bring them a little Wednesday-night joy to stave off any self-inflicted sad-sack shit, well then, watch me hop the ropes and fly.

I'm pacing in the belly of Sokol Auditorium. Slapping the concrete-walled hallways that work underneath and around and eventually lead to the center-set ring. Sokol has a stage and a balcony, and close to fifteen hundred people can cram in, max. Outside the squared circle, lean one way or the other too hard and you'll feel so many fingertips you might as well be the cutest goat at the petting zoo. The exterior of Sokol reads all church, with its brick facade and high, arching windows. A stone eagle also presents majestic above the entrance, with an actual cloth-and-dignity American flag waving overhead. Backstage is all business. A couple of rusty folding chairs. Banquet tables. A fruit plate. When we get the call, we emerge from behind a set of heavy purple drapes, a cheap programmable electric sign jerry-rigged to sway above us buzzing our names as the announcer calls us forward and the crowd roars. My name doesn't fit within the word limit, so it always reads RICKY2HAT, confusing the newcomers, because I'm not even wearing a hat.

Ricky Twohatchet is my name, although the government recognizes me as Richard Powell. I run half-Apache and half–Euro mutt: a mix of Irish, Scottish, and Polish. While fifty percent of the blood that courses through my veins is Native, I came out looking like I could model Scandinavian activewear. I'm naturally blond-haired, blue-eyed, with a smile so white it could run a Fortune 500 company. To help the sell, I dye my hair black twice a month at a boutique where the stylist can never shore up the sideburns, but she's a good listener and spends extra time on the complimentary shampoo, so I tip well. I also hit the tanning booth weekly, but that's more for muscle definition. Pops the lats. Lines the delts.

Seven years of making the rounds has led to this moment. From backyard wrestling to bar brawling in Seattle on a bunch of scummy mattresses to middling start-up conferences to this: I'm one level away from being one level away from the big leagues. And tonight is supposed to be my big hurrah. Here, in the belly of Sokol, surrounded by loved ones and onlookers ready to bear witness.

Only I've got to deal with 240 pounds of pissed-off Mexican before the ticker-tape parade.

Picture a preteen boy, sugar-sick off mainlining Mountain Dew, who spends too many hours on a video game and has amped all his character's stats to max to create this Uncanny Valley–looking cartoon version of a man shredded to the high heavens. That's Bojorquez. All brawn. He looks like he had back-alley surgery in Venezuela to fill all major muscle groups with motor oil. I only wish they were filled with fake fluid and weren't solid slabs forged by testosterone and effort.

I sidle up to the purple curtain, finger the folds. Wait for my cue. Under my breath, I say, "I am a tender man. I am a tender man. I am a tender man." My own little prayer cribbed from a quote by Mr. T about toughness. But don't peg me as a Bible thumper; prayer to me is only pleading words on air. Something we all have in common, whether you're Christian, Muslim, wide-eyed child, or wizard. *I am a tender man. I am a tender man. I am a tender man.*

Now, two ways generally exist to enter the ring. The slow go: the my-balls-are-so-big-I-have-to-walk-wide-legged-being-a-dude-so-endowed. Under deposition, Terry Bollea, better known as Hulk Hogan, said Hulk Hogan's dick is ten inches. Terry Bollea is not ten inches. Big difference. Flourishes include a finger point or a head turn toward different sections of the audience—always acknowledge the cheap seats. Or the full-out, Ultimate Warrior–perfected sprint so fast toward the ring that the announcer barely gets to finish your intro and there's zero chance the audience could Shazam your theme song. Sure there are other variations, but in general, there's fast and slow. Little in-between.

Now I'm back to full sprint. But I took a few years off. Switched tempo. Not out of any marketing gimmick; I was scared.

When I first started, seven years ago, I'd run hard, but once I slipped on a rubber, nonslip mat, skidded across the slick concrete, and ate it into the stairs. The audience gasped and I let out a weird little high-pitched yelp. Back then, I went by a different name, a whole different persona, so nobody except a handful of basement-dwelling, hard-core wrestling brains knew it was me when it went semiviral. This was also back when YouTube barely had walking legs, so viral then was about fifteen thousand hits. Still, the fewer people who know I was the "KISS THE STAIRS ZOMG!!!" guy, the better. It hasn't made it to Botcha-mania, a YouTube series that highlights wrestling fuckups or "botches," and for that I face Coral Gables and say a short prayer to the neon god, Macho Man, on a daily basis.

But I'm not scared anymore. I jaw on fear like bubble gum.

Once my music goes, I'm gone. No easy-does-it. Full-on adrenaline-dump run. "Run to the Hills" by Iron Maiden has a tough-talk last half, and these fans are not the type to reflect on their great-great-great-grandfather Clovis's role in slaying Natives during the New World migration west.

Cue the Maiden. I go running.

As I make my way ringside, one voice rises above all others. Frankie, my love, my dear, my heart, carrier of my kid. Frances Rae Dillashaw. Being from North Mississippi, she has a slight Southern lilt that is more pronounced when she's drunk and also when she lucks into decent Keno payouts. It floats above the din. Above the flat, nasal tones of my fellow fly-over crowd. Like a knob of butter on plain toast.

She is sporting denim overalls that I once accused her of wearing as a sarcastic knock at Midwesterners. Although she told me they were legit and that she was volunteering part-time at an urban farm, I've never even seen her cradle a rutabaga, so I'm skeptical. Still, she looks stunning in a white shirt and overalls.

Frankie is at every show. She's a support system, a lifeline. Even if she doesn't do signs.

"Where the hell do you put a sign when you're in the bathroom? While you're waiting in line for a hot dog?" she asked me once, mimed a whole routine where she wrestled with a poster board as big as a flatbed truck, and I never brought it up again.

Frankie is playing neighbors with Mom, because she's always next to Mom. They're so close they even have a secret handshake that involves kissing thumbs and a quick whisper to the wrestling gods that I emerge unhurt.

Arlene "Lena" Powell. One of those sports moms who show at their offspring's every game and wear their child's jersey along with some oversized sign or hat or other show of I'm-the-one-who-pushed-him-through-the-meat-curtains. The loudest to whoop and holler. She yells, "You've got this, Ricky! Kick their dicks in!" Usually in the vicinity of another parent covering her kid's ears with her hands from whatever else might come out of this strange lady's foul mouth; it's embarrassing, but that's Mom. You can't earmuff that kind of energy.

It's only been Mom and me for the past twenty-five years. Mano a momo. Pops is a goner. Never showed. Never mailed a card. Never phoned. Over the years I got accustomed to the seat beside her being empty, or else it was occupied by one of her latest dates. Few of the dudes cared enough to show, and if they did, it wasn't in good faith. None really tried. No attaboys. No positive-spin slogans. Life tells me I'm supposed to feel a pang of dad absence whenever I see that empty seat, but mostly I'm thinking, *Damn, that could've been a good place to rest a sign.* Maybe that's a deflect, but I prefer that alternative, otherwise I'd have to take on all two and a half decades of complicated dad abandonment issues, and sans therapy and popping pills it's easier to adopt the give-zero-fucks act.

When I make it to the ring, I hop up on the apron, center myself. I exhale loudly through my mouth, inhale through my nose for four seconds, hold my breath for seven seconds, and then exhale for eight seconds. It's a focusing technique Mom taught me. Next, I grip the top rope with both hands, and do a front flip into the ring to wild applause. A child could do it with the proper training, but it's a move that always wows. As they cheer, they can't hear me mutter to myself. I say my prayer and stomp down into the mat, because I need to feel grounded; I need to feel my weight in the balls of my feet. Something is off, though, because I don't feel the brunt of my body in my legs; everything below my knees feels floaty, like I sat down crisscross-applesauce-style for a long stretch and stood up right before stumbling out here.

Bojorquez comes out to mariachi music. All up-tempo brass and strings. He's dressed in his bad-guy getup: black tights, black boots, black pads, black bands. His hair slicked back into a wet ponytail. He used to wear brighter colors. More on the Roy G. Biv scale, in line with most Mexican wrestlers. Until his manager, Facundo, in an inspiration binge off peyote and old Mike Tyson YouTube videos, decided to redo Bojorquez's whole demeanor. Gives him the air of someone who does downtime at funerals. Goth jock vibe.

Before he even enters the ring, I snatch the mic from the announcer. Bojorquez's music comes to a halt. It's all preplanned, but he probably hates that the top brass okayed it. Bojorquez stops in his tracks fifteen feet from the edge of the ring. The audience noise simmers to a low roil. A few bold-faced drunkos scream obscenities at me. Tell me things they'd like to do with oblong fruit and my mother. It's expected. Bojorquez is the people's champ. He's been the reigning and defending king. I'm the new dude—fresh meat.

I'm hit with the spotlight; I clear my throat. "History lesson, folks. Apaches and Mexicans have had a long-standing hatred for each other. Before we knew the first names of every member of the extended Kardashians. Before 3D printers. Self-driving cars. That handsome mallard. Go way back. Sixteen hundreds to early nineteen hundreds. Three hundred years of warring. Bloodshed. Rivers and hills ran red. My people irked the Mexicans so much that the Mexican government even offered *mucho* pesos for an Apache scalp. Well, I'm here tonight to turn the tables," I say. "After I win, I'm coming for that head." I pull out a wig that looks like Bojorquez's, only it's a ratty renter that would never pass for his real sheen up close. It works for my purposes. I throw it on the ground. I stomp on it with my boot. The crowd loses it.

Bojorquez has heard enough. He comes flying full keel into the ring, and I see that Mexican meathead shoot at me with his forearm, the size of the barrel of a Louisville Slugger, aimed at my neck.

People always wonder how thick or thin between kayfabe and real life. Who really dislikes whom? Which marriages were even legal?

Which friendships were for show? Like in any other sport, fans love it when there's real dislike on the line. Tyson vs. Holyfield. Bulls vs. Pistons. Red Sox vs. Yankees. You can notch us up among the all-timers. Because Bojorquez fucking hates me.

Probably has to do with the fact that when Bojorquez and I first met backstage, six months ago, we had a minor miscommunication. It happened around a fruit plate. Donnie Deutch, our racist ringleader, for all his deep-seated hate, believes in the roster maintaining high Vitamin C levels. Not to pardon Donnie's dumb takes, but I never saw him actually treat anyone different. Hell, he keeps his roster stacked in absurd amounts of slightly bruised fruit. Figure he does back-alley delivery deals; probably pays high school kids to dumpster-dive for ditched Edible Arrangements. But he definitely gripes. He gripes every chance he gets to gripe, to anyone who is in the room. And they're always antiquated in nature. Donnie is like your racist uncle's racist uncle.

On this particular day, I kept pronouncing Bojorquez's name wrong. I'd throw a hard *J*, followed up with an even harder *Q*, and it came out "Bo-jork-quez." Then he'd say it right. Then I'd repeat it wrong. And on and on. Partly because I failed high school Spanish, and so I never wrapped my head around the subtleties of their tongue. Also because fuck him.

Truth is, I have no valid reason to dislike Bjork, except he and I have the same goals and it's easier to psych myself up by inventing overblown motives.

For those who might be wondering who's the heel and who's the face, the answer is we're both heels. Takes two to dance. If you're looking for a face, a do-gooder, someone as American as Superman swigging Coca-Cola with a bald eagle taloned on his arm, look no further than Johnny America. Big Boy Scout, Johnny Proper. He's a sunglasses-wearing, American-flag-pants-festooned goober. He smells like saddle leather and sweat. Comes out to the ring waving the Stars and Stripes to a backing track of Springsteen. You can't get more American than this motherfucker, except for the fact that he's actually German.

When I first made my way onto the Pro Magnum circuit, America was the first one who showed me the ropes. His real name is Johann Ammer, but I call him JA or America. America is actually a German immigrant who can only fake an American accent if he adopts a big Texas twang. He's only been in the States for five years but has such allegiances to the red, white, and blue way of life, he'll shout down anyone who doesn't stand correctly during the national anthem: full-on facing the flag with right hand flat over your heart. Even if his version of the American Dream is an old-timer's pipe dream, he believes so fervently, he decided to hop a plane at twenty-three with zip in the way of savings and fly to a city he randomly pointed to on a map. Wrestling is just a means to an end. He dreams of zany neighbors rushing into his oversized apartment in a nineties sitcom America.

After matches, we'd grab Double Pony Burgers or Pork Tenderloins at Bronco's. Drunk, we'd hit back nines at night or sneak into hotel swimming pools for quick dips. We were each other's emergency contacts. We lifted, ate, and practiced together.

He and I were tag-team champs and actually good buddies beyond kayfabe, but two weeks ago he was asked by higher-ups to take a new angle, and he was paired with Bojorquez. When we ran the tag-team division, we were known as the Trail of Terrors. When Bojorquez and America teamed up, they called themselves NATO: Naturally, Allies Take Over.

When he told me that he was going to have to screw me and switch sides, I was rightly upset. Business is business, but if Donnie wanted America on Bojorquez's side, he was saying something without saying something. It was a not-so-subtle dig to say, *You're not tops*. This was after weeks of them whispering in my ear that I was the next man up.

I'd been outselling Bojorquez and America and Roscoe Smoke 'Em and everyone else on the roster in merch. My tomahawks were flying like tomahawks. Plastic headdresses were popular. Not sure if the white kids who copped them were fans or folks who wanted to wear them to sweaty music festivals. T-shirts with my face and bold logo were draped as seat coolers in old Corollas all over Omaha. I was resonating, as they say. Or said.

Before the match, Bojorquez and I went over the ins and outs. Figured out what's going to happen to whom when. I told him to watch my neck. I'd been hit with a stinger two nights before and it was still a bit sore. Plan was I'd lose to Bojorquez after a fifteen-minute back-and-forth. Lots of action. Figuring out our spots. We'd set up a monthlong rivalry that'd lead to our big event, MagFest, which sounds like a convention for gun nuts. Right before we split to get things going, Johnny walked into the backstage area and told us that he's going to illegally ring Bojorquez with the bell. This will disqualify me, setting me up for MagFest, send some sympathy toward Bojorquez, and allow America to come back to my stable. We all agreed. Had a handshake deal.

But now, in the ring, I'm questioning everything. Not only the wrestling-related. I mean every turn, every door, every meal order that led me here, staring at this behemoth of a dude who is so yoked that it looks like his kneecaps have abs. I'll be fine in the larger, cosmic sense. But there's no guarantee he doesn't put a little extra on his punches. No matter what, I have to sell them. This is my time to deliver.

Only, our flow is all off. Sometimes you grip a hand, kiss a girl, high-five a stranger, and it all goes wrong. Like in another dimension, you have aced it, but this version of you is two beats late, an inch left. There's a natural ebb but very little flow. Kicks, flips, ropewalks, flying splashes. Our two styles should mesh well. But it's no classic. No Macho Man vs. Steamboat. Hitman vs. Heartbreak Kid. But we're doing our part to appease the greasy patrons. Bojorquez really sells the chest slaps. Rings my ear for real with an elbow to the head. I reverse his hold, send him flying across the ring into the ropes. What we do was long ago repackaged as sports entertainment. It is now universally acknowledged that the end results are arranged. But it's still murder on the body. Cactus Jack getting his ear ripped off. Droz getting paralyzed after being dropped on his head. Sid Vicious snapping his leg. Sometimes you get a weird sense that there's a bullet with your name on it, a supernatural nod that you're next. I feel that shiver deep in my bowels when I Irish Whip Bojorquez for the third time and see Johnny America crawl into the ring with the bell in tow.

You know those old fogeys who watch the same whodunits and expect to find different culprits? They'd be the only audience surprised to find I'm fucked. There is no hitting Bojorquez. I'm the target. And although I don't think Johnny means to make as much contact as he does, the bell rings me good. So much so, I jerk and hear something snap in my neck. When I go down, I actually black out for a few seconds. When I come to, I hear a scream from a stranger that's so loud, the response is instant silence. People can tell this is no act. I broke something. Bojorquez stops. Johnny lets the bell drop. Facedown on the canvas, I try to move my neck, but I'm in so much pain that I'm sure I'm paralyzed. The ref calls it. Bojorquez's mariachi music gets cued in to cover up the silence. The rest is Vaseline over my memory. The shock numbs me crazy, and I try to wiggle my pinkie toes, because I saw it in a movie once. Mom and Frankie are in the ring and asking what the hell is wrong with my ankles, because my feet keep doing weird flexes and points like a bad ballerina, and I say, "My pinkie toes! They won't move," and Frankie has the wherewithal to tell me that almost no one can wiggle their pinkie toes. Paramedics rush to my side with a stretcher. They turn me over and snap a temporary brace on. I'm lifted by four men in blue polos and powder-blue latex gloves. As I'm wheeled out, I'm almost dropped, so they have to lift me and right me again. As I'm taken away, I see Johnny America out of the corner of my eye. He gives me this bullshit grimace and tries to touch my hand. I scream, "Fuck you, America! Fuck you!" as loud as I can. Adrenaline courses through my body. I'm spitting, I'm so amped. One of the paramedics puts his hand on my chest and tells me to calm down. I keep screaming until they wheel me into the ambulance. People have their phones out, documenting the whole ordeal.

The clip goes viral. Not the injury or the aftermath, just the ten seconds of me being wheeled out screaming the F-bomb at America. Without context, it looks bad, very bad.

Talk radio jockeys call for my deportation. TMZ labels me "The Commie Kid." A GoFundMe is started to buy me a one-way ticket to North Korea. Then a week later, a pop star gets caught with her hands down the pants of a model in front of a group of disabled Disneyland kids and it's all anyone can talk about. The world spins on.

Pro Mag gives me the pink slip, although it's less a pink slip and more of an all-caps email with lots of exclamation points. Donnie throws in a couple of outdated slurs that might be racist, but I'm in no mood to Google, so I let them slide.

Because of the injury, I also have to alert my full-time job. Even though high school graduation has long been in my rearview, I still get nervous thinking about marching to the principal's office. Back when I was a young runt, I was one of those bad-news kids, meaning they'd call my mom and the first words out of their mouths were "Bad news . . ." So I still feel sweat form across my brow, in that valley right above my butt cheeks while I sit, uncomfortable, in one of three pleather chairs outside of Principal McWhorter's office. Keep shifting my position, because I'm still learning how to sit in this neck contraption. Her office isn't even one of those where the bigwig is a vague shadow behind a door with an ominous frosted-glass window. Today all the offices are floor-to-ceiling glass, so I can see her sitting in there, checking her email and flossing her teeth. But that still doesn't ease the flow of butt sweat. The chestnut it feels like I'm trying to swallow when they call my name.

CHAPTER TWO

I'M A CUSTODIAN at my alma mater, Benson High—go Bunnies. That's right, bunnies. To be fair, we're the Mighty Bunnies, but that adjective only invites even worse burns. Especially in an online culture of smart asses with a passing aptitude in Photoshop. Nick Nolte is a famed alumnus, so there's that. I've been working at the school for the past few months since I resettled in Omaha. Before that, having to hit the road so much, I was mostly working in the service industry: serving and tending bar. But after I signed with Pro Mag and settled into my own city, I picked up a job with more stability.

Only now I have to tell them that I need a leave of absence, because I can't move my neck to check out my own ass.

Not sure why the nerves. Principal McWhorter has always been kind, but it's still a grating-on-your-self-esteem thing to ask an authority figure for extended time off, even if it's got to be done. Capitalism has bamboozled us to feel bad if we have to step back from the daily grind; hard work is equated with our self-worth, or that's approximately what Mom texts me the morning I go in to deliver the news.

I walk into Principal McWhorter's office and take a seat. It's only the third time I've ever even been inside. Pretty typical: framed photos of a nuclear family, JV soccer trophies, various badges and awards. Inspirational posters, but with mixed messages. One has a photo of a young man dunking, and he's wearing one of those infant-strapped-to-his-chest deals, and it appears like he's threatening to blow this shit up, but his ammo is nine pounds of chunky baby. It says, *Don't Let Pregnancy Stop You from Making a Slam Dunk!* Which seems like a dick thing to say to a kid. Also, pregnancy has never stopped anyone from dunking a basketball ever. I'm chewing on all this when McWhorter speaks up.

"Ricky? I heard you wanted to talk," McWhorter says, blinks back tears from just applying eyedrops. Dabs at the corners of her eyes with tissue. I'm hoping the fake tears will somehow make her more empathetic.

"I'm pretty sure you can guess where this is headed," I say, a reminder of a bruise still on my cheek. Me motioning to my neck work with the flourish of a gameshow host offering up a consolation prize.

Principal McWhorter stands average height for a woman her age, I'd say, a little shrunk due to life's burdens, but she has Big Diction Energy. Her voice fills a room. And not in a phony baritone, because surveys show men respect the deeper boom more, like that blood-vial-scamming CEO. Hers is a genuine blast from the diaphragm.

She's so kind. Not sure why I had any doubts. I figured they'd just fire me, but I've built a strong bond with the students and do my work in a timely fashion and with a reasonable level of professionalism. When I first started, I thought a custodial job would mostly involve sweeping, wiping, and trash collecting. Turns out there's so much more. I'm cleaning ceiling vents, stripping and sealing floors, shampooing carpets. Helping students and teachers with messes. I'm not Mary Poppins on the corners, not white-glove cleaning the place, but it's clean enough.

Clean if you look at it cross-eyed. Only I can't do any of that now, when my spine and neck aren't on speaking terms.

"I completely understand," she says.

McWhorter stands to hug me, her pregnant belly bumping into my flat stomach. It's awkward—she's shorter, I'm taller, she's pregnant, my neck is in a bind. "Don't forget to leave a note for your kids," she says. "And contact us when you're better."

My kids are the Intertribal Council. I wouldn't go so far as to say I'm a mentor, but I'm an adult in their corner, and sometimes that's enough. The Intertribal Council is a group of Native kids that I've befriended, and I don't want them to think I up and left without a word, so I leave a note in their room that I hope the other custodians don't accidentally trash. I could Snapchat it to them, but I'm pretty sure they'd never speak to me again.

Pilgrim is their leader. I feel a kinship with the kid, because he also looks white. Pilgrim is one of those kids who looks thirty-five at eighteen. The Rock in high school wearing a sport coat and sporting a thin mustache. Looks like an undercover cop. That's Pilgrim. Swap the mustache for a little chin-strap beard. Wears a beanie no matter the temp. Big body; I'd say at least six foot on the low end and almost two fifty. But a baby face. And gentle. Real even keel. Probably why he's their head honcho.

I met Pilgrim and crew one day after regular school hours; I got a call that there was a malfunctioning computer projector in a classroom. I know jack shit about hardware, but the audio/video teach was gone for the day.

I walked into the classroom and saw seven students sitting in a circle. All dark-haired, except one had yellowish-dyed hair that came out more orange. Boys and girls in intense talk. Couldn't really peg any of them as belonging to one crew, whether they swayed nerd, jock, goth.

Although I think those hard-line distinctions only really exist anymore in movies about high school. INTERTRIBAL COUNCIL is what it said on the whiteboard. My people. Only I didn't want to lead with that.

"You need help with the projector?" I asked.

"Yeah, it's acting up," one boy said. He stood to the side of it. Tapped at it with his fingers. He wore a Chicago Bulls hat. Had gauged ears.

"I'm not tech savvy, but I'm the only guy on-site who can help you, so I'll give it a shot," I said.

I poked around, pretended I knew what I was doing. Caught little bits of the kids' conversations. Shit-talk about homework. Sports banter.

I unplugged. Pushed buttons. Plugged it back in. No dice.

"Let me get you guys a laptop that you can use to project whatever you need to," I said.

"Guys?" one of the girls asked.

I shuffled off before she launched into that convo. I grabbed one of the laptops stored in the A/V room. Wiped it off. Tucked it under my arm like I was a businessman with a very important portfolio.

"What are y'all watching?" I asked.

"*Thunderheart*," said Bulls boy.

"Isn't that with Val Kilmer?"

"Yes."

"I'm your huckleberry," I said, made a finger gun and then twirled it into my imaginary holster.

"What?"

"I'm your huckleberry."

"You're my what?"

"Here's your laptop," I said, handed it to the Bulls fan.

"Very white of you sir," he said, gave me a firm handshake. The whole crew laughed.

"Go easy on him, Jacob," Pilgrim said, bailing me out. Gave me a nod.

I'd run into Pilgrim on a regular basis before meetings. When he'd be setting up, either talking with the teacher who had to act as liaison, or in there by himself, booting up a computer or stacking napkins next to a box of Krispy Kremes.

"No way, you're half, too?" Pilgrim asked me once, a few weeks in. "Join the club." Then he dapped me up.

We shot the shit about life. I gave him the rundown about Frankie. The baby. Wrestling. I showed him a couple of my clips on YouTube. Not me doing the dumb-ass slide into the steps, though. He told me about how he was also the child of a single mother. Got held back a year because he was quiet and a second-grade teacher thought he was slow.

I got to know a few others: Jacob and Tara and Eileen. Chicago Bulls boy is Jacob. Jacob Grey Cloud. Kid is stylish. He's always wearing a different NBA cap. Favors a throwback Denver Nuggets lid with the rainbow and the mountains. Always shouldering one of those Swedish backpacks with the red fox logo. A bit standoffish.

Tara is the second-in-command. The smartest in the room, me included, but does that passive thing where whenever she speaks, she looks up and away like there's a cue-card holder feeding her the best lines. She's the one with the bad blonde dye job. Rocks a lot of piercings. Parts I didn't even know you could pierce. A cheek. The weird connective tissue on the inside of her mouth. A random part of her elbow.

Eileen is her best friend or girlfriend or no-label confidante. Tight-knit in that particular way where half their convo is inside jokes that are completely unintelligible to anyone not in the know. Sometimes even a sound—a stutter, a cough, a half-said word—sets them off into uncontrollable laughing fits.

I hope they haven't seen the news. Although I definitely feel like they would think better of me for it. No one at school has given me any guff, has made any mention of it; apparently since I'm not faculty and the parents don't know me, no one has floated the administration any angry emails asking for my termination due to bad-mouthing America.

I take in the room. I'll miss them; miss this. The camaraderie. The smack talk. I smell cleaning solution for the whiteboards. But then I breathe too hard and the hurt flashes between my ribs, so I take a couple of short, stuttering ones. And almost collapse. Have to grab the back of a chair for balance. I'd never live it down if the kids found my passed-out body all prone, with a soft-ass good-bye note crumpled in my fist.

CHAPTER THREE

EVERY BREATH IS a knife to the spine. I can barely bend over. Four screws in my neck tether together this garbage bag of a body. Pre-accident, one might say I was physically peak me. Twenty-five years old. Cut enough to sculpt that weird V line where your abs high-five your obliques. But what good is keeping something tuned up only to have it break down? Also, the shit whip on top of the turd pie is that I have to wear a cervical collar. Everything between my chin and shoulders reads half-robot. Not like the old cartoon neck braces that were little more than a giant wrap—swaddle that neck beef-and-bean-burrito-style. Before I left the hospital, the doctor handed me a gallon of milk. Told me to lift it. Said not to lift anything heavier. Handed me a pamphlet about "body mechanics." Got me on my way.

Showering is an awkward display of taking angles; although I don't have to wear the gear inside the tub, I do because it makes me feel safer, so the thing gets soaked. Smells like mildew and feet. Pissing is also a long shot. Aim in the general direction and hope not to hit the back of the lid and have my piss splash back at me. Not being able to bend your neck is all about having blind faith in the world. Anything below waist level is a guessing game. The trash can in my room has more discarded tissues on the floor than in the actual can; it looks like I've got a weak jumper.

Bills come in from the hospital. Numbers so large that they seem comical to me. Box-office big. Okay, indie box office, tops. I stop opening them.

I have two hundred and seventeen dollars in my bank account, and I'm unemployed.

Thing about making a living off your body is that once it's impossible to engage in basic functions like walking normally, eating normally, and shitting normally, much less take in a paycheck, you cast doubt on how you spend your days. Every action takes so much labor that you second-guess whether it's necessary. Which then leads you to question who you are. If not a wrestler, at least I was a stand-up son, boyfriend, possible father. But I barely have time to consider my condition; no mental skipping through the peonies or daydreaming at vistas, because Frankie lays the boom on me.

She texts me: *i did it got gelato after*

We were pregnant. Well, she was pregnant, but I've heard that modern dudes take partial ownership of the pregnancy. We. Not sure if that's forward or backward thinking. I wasn't the one who was going to be saddled with stretch marks. Going to have to whip out a tit for Ricky Junior. Deal with maternity clothes that didn't so much accentuate the right parts as they did sneak everything else.

I wanted the kid. Wanted to be the upstanding dad my deadbeat never was. Wanted to earn those *#1* mugs and aprons and cards.

"We can't have a kid right now, Ricky," Frankie had said to me. "We're both struggling." She was squirreling away money to enroll in classes at the local community college, because she wanted to get her degree in

American Sign Language. Transition into helping the hearing-impaired in social work.

This was three weeks ago in her studio apartment, when she was staring at multiple positive pregnancy tests lined up on the kitchen counter. It was a ratty little renter with cigarette smoke–yellowed walls. One of her neighbors would fall asleep watching bad horror flicks on full volume, and she could hear the title screens playing on repeat all night. Machete-wielding masked men haunted her dreams. She paid for her apartment by working sixty-plus hours a week serving at two different Midtown restaurants. Her patrons were old folks who dropped pretty pennies on prime Nebraska beef, but refused to shake any extra change to the help. Once she even got a tip line that was filled in with the words: *You chose this life.*

She settled into her thinking chair, a big, faded, gray recliner that her dad had used. She pulled her red UNO hooded sweatshirt over her legs. Cinched closed the top; spoke out of the tiny head hole.

"Why not? The numbers?" I said. I sat across from her, used a gross spoon to scrape microwaved macaroni off the edges of a hot-sided bowl. *Breaking Bad* on in the background.

"You say that like it's not real. Like money isn't real," Frankie said.

"Is it real, though?"

"Yes. I have to touch it every day. Every day."

"But can you touch it, though? Not paper. What the paper represents."

"The economy?"

"Exactly," I said, gestured at my temple with the spoon. A piece of macaroni hung off it like it was a tiny phone the spoon was using. "So sorry to interrupt your call, sir."

"Don't call me 'sir,'" Frankie said.

We had our way of joking through things, but fact was we weren't going to agree. It didn't have anything to do with religion or belief in life over choice or me thinking since I was the man that my say should have more sway. I actually had no clue I wanted to be a dad until the germ of that idea was planted in my head. It was like not knowing square watermelons existed and then wanting to eat nothing but square watermelons for the rest of your life.

She didn't want the baby. I wanted the baby. I told her she had to do what she deemed best, but I said that it was going to hurt me, it was going to rip me apart. And not like rip or hurt me in the way a vagina would rip or hurt when giving birth to new life, but in the way that the vagina of my heart would rip in doing the opposite of that. She laughed. I didn't.

I knew she was dead set on her decision, but that she did it on a whim, or at least without fully consulting me before the actual act, definitely burned. Really, I thought I had more time. More time to convince her otherwise. Wishful thinking, but a silver lining after the injury was the idea that I could look forward to us possibly having the kid. Who knows what rehab offers me in the way of wrestling, but no matter what, my career has an end point. You can't be a lifelong ballerina, because your body will break down. Same thing. Maybe my next move was dad. Better than my long-lost, deadbeat one. Fucking hall-of-fame dad. Personalized pancakes made with a squeeze bottle. Front row at every public performance. Nightly tuck-ins. The whole package. But when I got the text, all that was gone.

CHAPTER FOUR

I MET FRANKIE at an improv comedy class. This was two years prior to even getting eyes from Pro Mag. I was still a baby in the game, and my mic skills and general witticisms left much to be desired. Luckily, I was bouncing around in no-name circuits, and sometimes we'd be wrestling to a threesome of people who only paid because they thought it was an open-mic night and they needed cheap drinks in a dark place. I knew I needed help when, once, after I got done shouting a half-assed promo into the mic, an old man with tattooed roses across both hands and a sword across his throat stood up and mimed sucking a dick, saying, "Stop swallowing the mic, champ." That was in the basement of a punk club in Akron, Ohio.

During a temporary hiatus from hitting the road, I came back home to Omaha and signed up for improv and sketch comedy classes. I felt like they could help me work the crowd. Be at ease on the big stage. Come quicker off the top. And I still owe all my slick-talk savvy to that class: getting out of speeding tickets, off-the-cuff call-in-sick excuses, every crowd-applauded monologue I launched in the ring.

First day, Enid, a twentysomething woman who dressed like she was in her sixties, led us in ice-breaker exercises. She wore baubles, trinkets, costume jewelry. She looked like a child playing dress-up from her grandma's armoire; the jewelry was a few decades out of style. She also wore big, square-lensed glasses, and when they slipped off her small nose, she'd constantly push them back up with her first finger. She led us in Follow the Leader; Story, Story, Die!; and The Johnson File.

The group was twelve people of mixed races, ages, genders, and haircuts, stuffed into a dark classroom in a nondescript building that doubled as a community service center. Some nights we'd stroll past the next group shuffling in with their looks of shame, delinquents sitting through anger-management sessions or stop-sign runners looking to strike a ticket from their record. Our crew looked like a group of patients in an ad for dialysis. Micah was a plumber from a legacy of plumbers. Loretta was a Black, forty-year-old mother of two, who secretly had Hollywood aspirations of being an extra on *Empire*, and only did improv as a way to decompress from her day job and night classes. Kensington, or Kensey, as she'd rather have us call her, wanted to move to Chicago and become a member of Second City. She had been a popular cheerleader at her high school, but she'd rather hang with the drama geeks and work on YouTube skits. Then there was Frankie.

Frances Rae, but we could call her Frankie. She was quick. She got the biggest laughs. Not even for the punch lines so much as her natural timing and sincerity in each scene. She was also pretty in a way that was new to me. Later, she told me her dad was Irish-Swedish and her mom was Black-Creole. Frankie had light skin, curly blonde hair, and freckles, but she wasn't what most dopes would look at and finger as white. What I'd call her is a rare beauty; stats show every pretty kid in the future will look like Frankie, but those fetuses fucking wish. Frankie and I gravitated toward each other like two little kids who are wearing the same superhero shirt the first time they meet. The moment we held hands for this group exercise, I felt a sizzle in the air that was more likely a mix of sweat and pheromones and static electricity. But I knew we were going to fuck. And fall in love. And tear each other apart. And all the other dumb shit two incredibly good-looking people thrumming with sexual tension are bound to get wrapped up in. I was up for everything short of manslaughter.

"We're back, Chet. I'm here courtside with Magnus Michaelson. He's just won the Grand Slam for the first time. Michaelson, how are you feeling after such a historic match?"

Enid was yelling me along, telling me to dig deep. I wore a blond wig, a sportscaster's coat from the seventies with different-colored elbow patches. The skit was an interview between an analyst and an egotistical athlete. Enid put me in the sportscaster role. Micah wore a headband and held an old catgut tennis racket. I lost it. My voice went hoarse and a vein in my neck flexed from my effort, itching for the spotlight.

Micah went full McEnroe, playing the diva. He delved into non sequiturs and one-liners. He kept deep sighing into the "camera" and looking at me side-eyed. I pushed it up a notch.

"Well, Magnus, I can see the stink lines. I'd throw to Chet in studio, but we've got another thirty seconds to burn, so tell me, do you have a problem with me, Magnus? Me and you?" I pushed his arm up so that the racket was now between our faces like a mini-barrier. "Here, bucko, you're a religious man, right? Imagine this is you sitting stupid in confession. What's the deal, bud?"

Micah was thrown off. He didn't know what to do. He broke for a second, gave Enid a shrug. I knew he was mine. Enid rolled her hands as if to say, *Keep going with it.*

"C'mon, Magnus, the home audience wants to know. You got a problem?" I took the racket with both hands and slammed my head through the cheap strings. It hung around my head like a tribal necklace. I was bleeding, with long scratches at the edges of my face. Micah just blinked at me. Enid was clapping. Someone else screamed out. I heard a "Holy shit!" Frankie was laughing hard.

She also gave me a nod, a sly smile. She didn't want to, but I could tell. Enid was screaming, "Yes! Yes! Yes!" in the background.

Classes finished. In a final flourish, Enid showed up on the last day, but not as the Enid we knew. She looked like your regular underclassman. She had her hair pulled back into a ponytail and she was wearing a navy blazer. Gone were the baubles, the trinkets, the chains. Gone were the granny glasses. She looked her demographic. It turned out it was a whole act. All the affectation was gone. She'd been playing pretend. Some people covered their mouths. Kensey gasped. Micah stood up, near in tears, yelled, "I thought we had something. I introduced you to my hamster." Enid bowed.

Frankie agreed to a first date. Didn't so much agree as we found ourselves after the last class, the last two left drunk at the bar, making out like high school kids on this bus bench. Later, we still cited it as the first date, because what's a first date? Two soft bodies getting hard? A certain time spent smelling the breath of a stranger? I've seen people on a date not break eye contact with their own glowing phone. I've seen a grown man in a coffee shop meet-cute with a stuffed animal. All I knew was post–bus bench, there was an us.

CHAPTER FIVE

FRANKIE WOULD MAKE a great mom. Puts up with my antics. Firm but kind in her rebukes. Has that psychic foretelling ability that all good parents possess. Tells you to grab a banana when you didn't even know you were hungry. Even saved my life after I almost died from a day hike.

Omaha has a sad excuse for a skyline. Should be ashamed to be on a license plate. Not really scraping the sky so much as skirting it. Regardless of being vertically challenged, the city is spread out. Ever since my childhood, Omaha has grown farther west and north. But not in any interesting ways. Chain stores. Model homes. The usual.

Neale Woods is this refuge in the middle of all this urban sprawl. Near the Ponca Hills, you can drop a five-spot on any weekday to go hug a tree and walk well-maintained trails for a few hours. It loops around and doesn't require that much energy. Wildflowers and prairie brush surround the pathways, but the main thoroughfares are all tamped-down grass or pebble walkways or wooden boards. Easy on the ankles. It's like getting in touch with nature if you barely want to touch nature. People are always taking engagement photos during high-traffic times.

Frankie and I went one day because we were bored and tired of staring at our phones. So we paid the fiver, parked, and hoofed the trails.

This was early on. When we hadn't really talked about what we were, but we'd definitely slept over at each other's places and started to sketch out what type of people we'd shown our privates.

"Tell me more about your mom," she said. She noticed Mom and I were close.

I filled her in on the single-mother child-rearing details. Homemade haircuts. Sometimes cereal for dinner. Most of my toys were Happy Meal and box-top freebies.

"No dad?" she asked.

"You can't just go around asking people about their dads," I said.

"You're right, I'm sorry. Your other mom?" Frankie asked, twirled a stick she'd found.

"No, no others."

Frankie laid out her background: typical lovey-dovey stuff. Supportive parents. Mother was a cardiologist; father was an econ professor. Married for twenty-seven years. She mentioned how she thought she was queer or at least questioning when she was thirteen and she cried to her father, who held her like a child in his office and told her they'd always have her back.

"And your other mom?" I asked. She hit me with the stick, snapped it in half. "Also, don't take this the wrong way, but how did your parents come from such esteemed backgrounds and then saddle their daughter with a name that sounds like it belongs to the lady silhouette on mud flaps?"

"It's my great-grandmother's name. Also, Richard Powell? The prime suspect in every *SVU* episode. Excuse me, excuse me, Ricky. What are you, a NASCAR driver?" We both faked our hurt, laughed at our stupid needling. I blew dandelion seeds in her direction.

That day there were two sets of people getting their photos taken for future engagement announcements. Two women dressed in tailored suits I could never pull off and a future husband-and-wife duo that were cosplaying medieval era chain mail. But elegant. Not like sex dungeon.

The husband and wife were set up on a prime trail spot, so I convinced Frankie to take a detour.

"Let's do the right thing," I said.

"But we have to veer through that high grass," she said.

"Neither of us are wearing basketball shorts, so we're fine."

Only I didn't actually want to get too sidetracked. I went just enough out of our way that I knew I was likely to be in the viewfinder of the photographer, because the best scenery was behind us. I jumped up and struck an athletic pose like I was running midair. Then I leapt again as high as I could and pulled a Jumpman: arms out and legs splayed like Jordan.

"What the hell are you doing?" Frankie asked.

"Trying to get in the background of these photos," I said.

"They won't print the ones of the idiot pretend-dunking in the background," she said.

"Says you," I said.

"C'mon."

"One more pose."

But when I leapt the last time, I must've hit a mud spot or some other wetness and I screamed as I went tumbling into a bunch of loess. Rolled little-kid style, picking up debris with me. I lay there for a few minutes, not wanting to get up out of embarrassment. Closed my eyes. "Leave me," I said, when Frankie tried to help me up.

Frankie laughed and laughed and laughed. She picked the ticks off that had buried themselves in my arms. Twisted a few stragglers free that had gotten underneath my jeans.

She even drove me to the hospital three days later, when I was staying over at her place and she noticed that I was sweating and convulsing. I didn't pee for two days and felt like my kidneys were shutting down. She drove me to the emergency room, and when the nurse asked me my symptoms and I responded, she straight-up asked me if I had HIV. In front of Frankie. Turned out I had a one-in-two-million tick bite from a Rocky Mountain breed that wasn't even supposedly in Nebraska, and one had sunk its head deep into the soft spot behind my knee. Luckily, it wasn't the Lyme disease or make-me-allergic-to-meat type, but I felt like I was going to die for a few days, and Frankie nursed me through them. Most people are afraid to fart in front of a loved one. I had the shakes, soiled her bed with leaks, and was asked point-blank if I was HIV positive in front of her, which is no knock on those who are, but not the way you want to break it to your date. She still stuck it out, which was why I knew she was golden.

CHAPTER SIX

THAT SHE WOULD text me after the abortion was done is so her.

She probably really did get the gelato, but there's no doubt she's devastated in her own way. I know it's no easy decision. She didn't go in whistling and kick her feet into the stirrups. Hell, I'm not even sure of the machinery, the layout of the room. And I'm not saying it was a breeze for her emotionally, either.

One night after our initial convo about her positive pregnancy tests, she called me late. She had an early shift, so she stayed at her place, but she buzzed me at two a.m., sleep in her voice.

"What if we did do it?" she asked. The "it" so important, but dropped as casually as an ice cream order.

"What's it?"

"I mean, have the baby . . ." she said, but trailed off. Not a pause for effect, but an actual fall-asleep cliffhanger. But I think that was dream brain talking and not waking brain, so I didn't want to bring it up again. If anything, I was going to let her initiate that conversation, but she never directly made mention of it until I got the text that it was done, so that was that.

Still, I'd be lying if I didn't feel this deep cleaving. I imagine the undone baby as a girl, for some reason. I imagine it one-half white, one-quarter Native, and one-quarter Black-Creole, if that math even checks out. Probably would've had the prettiest eyes. Like blue marbles dipped in molasses. I would've bathed her in the kitchen sink. Kissed the bottoms of her tiny feet. This kind of thinking isn't healthy, but it's how I'm coping. I feel the pain deep in my spleen. I feel like my heart got an elbow off the top rope.

When she texted, I was driving and couldn't check it immediately. I had to meet Mom at Mulhall's to help her pick out succulents. No heavy lifting, per doctor's orders, solely second opinion giving. Mulhall's is a large-scale nursery with ornate patio furniture and terrariums for sale with plants wedged up everything's ass. Imagine eco-friendly IKEA. You don't know if you're getting sold plants or woven baskets, but the trick is both in combo. Visual merchandising team probably thought millennials would read a plant-plus-wicker set as a surefire sign of maturity. Every woman I know owns more than five houseplants, and every dude I know hasn't used a headboard past the age of seven. Mom asked to get me out of the house. She also said plants promote healing. Help us breathe. Didn't have the guts to tell her yet that whatever greenery we choose better be for her house, because I barely had enough scratch to survive another month in my apartment.

Mom was checking out. Had her arms around a pair of begonias (she wasn't awed by the succulent selection) she was nestling like they were her new favorite kids. I caught some downtime and read the text. Even though it was less than ten words. I had an inkling it was coming, but again, I was shocked it came so soon. I had to excuse myself and found a corner behind some large rhododendrons and quietly sniffled, my head hangdog. Had to tilt my whole upper half weird because of the brace and brushed by too close, caught some leaves in the machinery. I heard the young clerk with an orange neckerchief and one of those painted-on beauty marks ask Mom if I was all right.

"Allergies," Mom said. After she checked out, she came over to me, rubbed my shoulders, and led me to the parking lot. "Go home, get some rest. Call me if you need anything." Mom went to hug me, but I was too raw. Needed to be alone. I pulled back. "I love you, Ricky," she said. "Here, take one of these. It'll brighten up your kitchen." She handed me one of the begonias.

I drove the entire way to my apartment without realizing I never put the begonia inside my car. A few flecks of dirt on the roof the only evidence a plant ever existed. Probably got ten or fifteen feet before that thing went sky-bound. Hope it landed gracefully in a patch of open soil to grow another few decades into its final form. Some redwood or whatever. I don't know how nature works. Realistically, it's probably tire mulch, crushed before it even got a shot.

CHAPTER SEVEN

I'M BACK AT home. Here to stay, no pit stop. And by "home," I mean Mom's. The place where I was raised.

Previously, I had a little studio apartment that was in a low-income block housing half Burmese refugees and half people heavy into illegal extracurriculars. Neighbors who added real color. Rita, an old white woman with no front teeth, who always wore faded eighties exercise gear, would pass by me and mutter things under her breath, which I imagined were trailer park curses. But to what end, I'm not sure. Maybe I was meant to wake up the next day with skin bleached into the color of juggalo face paint. Or my pantry would be chock-full of Larry the Cable Guy–brand chips, but only Ketchup and Tater Salad flavors. After my accident I couldn't pay my bills, so I borrowed money from Mom to pay them off and then moved back in with her.

Mom's plot is a little postage stamp off the strip in Benson. Benson now is cocktail bars where everything is served in a snifter, rooftop patios where West O yuppies meet for margs, three different shiny music venues, and a DIY garage where shy poets read their sad tweets off their phones. But old-school Benson folks, living right off the strip, are leading very different lives. Families who regularly call one another by their first names and share kiddie pools and mowers. Pick up after each other's pets and help with courtesy sidewalk snow clearing.

Mom's is a brick-exterior, two-story number that looks like it'd be the logo for a carpet-cleaning service: it's that clear-cut, middle-class American. Even with the white trim. Omaha is hilly as hell, so the yard slants at a steep angle that makes mowing murder for anyone without decent triceps and legs. I did it for years, but since I moved out, I think she pays a neighborhood kid to pick up the slack. Inside is all maroon carpeting and three upstairs bedrooms, but I live and lived off the main kitchen. We call it the extra-large bathroom. Not because people take shits in there, but because my room is right off the kitchen, where one would naturally expect there to be a restroom.

Nothing's changed. Room still has the same sour air scent. Same *Back to the Future* posters with peeling corners. Same Ric Flair and Macho Man action figures. Roughshod dioramas and science projects. Stacks of skateboarding mags. Everything coated in dust. Circles mar the carpet where the hue gets a hint darker. We once owned a coonhound that lasted three months. A neighbor gave him to me out of a cardboard box. The thing pissed and vomited so frequently in my room, the stains left reminders. We had to ditch the dog to a better home and garden. Better for both parties.

They say you can't go home again, but who the fuck are "they"? They probably didn't go viral for getting listed on the *Huffington Post*'s top twenty anti-American moments, slotted only seventeen behind 9/11.

Mom also convinces me to move back, because I have very few options and she has a lot of downtime, like all the time. Because she doesn't work. Doesn't need to.

Mom paid her dues in the public high school system as a staff member for years and then spent a little over a decade working as a cashier for this mom-and-pop pizzeria; five years ago, Sal, the owner, ended up selling to a corporate pizza chain. Shortly after, when Sal passed, he wrote Mom into his will. She probably knew him more than his own kids. Stayed late, came in early. Talked him through the heartbreak of losing his wife to stomach cancer. Mom ended up getting almost three hundred thousand. Paid off her home, and still had a nice stack left. Didn't do anything grand with it, just wanted to sit on it and use it to give her the freedom she didn't have in her early years. Salad days, she'd say, which I thought meant when we were so poor, she'd have to eat leftover salads from work.

So I'm home. No job. Neck got me straight-backed like an elementary school chair. I'm in it for another three to four months. Days, I sit stolid on my old sheets. Stare at Netflix binges and eat my way into two pants sizes higher. Reason being? I still eat like calories drip off me, but now they stick around, make friends, multiply.

I was a top-tier athlete for most of my life. Blessed with freak-level metabolism. I could down half a ham hock and run a marathon backward. I played sports—you name it: football, basketball, tae kwon do, swimming, track, wrestling from the age of five until now. I was always athletic. And when you burn calories like that, you ingest them with no regard for casualties. Short story short: my eating habits stay the same, and I pack on the pounds. Suddenly, nothing sounds more sacred than bread. Except bread drenched in eggs, cinnamon, and milk and fried in butter. Topped with powdered sugar. A few slices of banana for potassium. Covered in maple syrup. I could go on.

Sweatpants become my go-to for ease of peeing. Those extra seconds of fumbling with a button and a zipper are extra seconds of self-reflection that my brain can't process. Immediately after the surgery, Mom had the top-tier job of having to unzip and pull my pants down for me for any major bathroom breaks. I did all the messy work; she just had to assist in the prep. That lasted for about three days until we both realized sweatpants were the way to go. I can drop trou by myself with little effort. Although, to get me back for the awkwardness of those seventy-two hours, Mom walks by me when I'm standing at the fridge or doing something else right-side up and yanks at my sweatpants: middle-of-the-kitchen pantsed. It's her way of retribution.

"Mom, I think I have to break things off with Frankie," I say while we're doing yoga to Internet videos broadcast big on the TV. Mom doesn't want to fork over the cash for real lessons. Hell, the top-flight brands of pants alone are criminal. She has the cash, but years of single-parent living will instill those frugal moves until death does she part.

She wears sweats and one of my old basketball jerseys. Vintage Shawn Kemp, Supersonics green, although the colors have faded and bled a bit. I'm doing the things I can do. Getting the most work from my waist, hips, knees, and feet. Going hard on everything south of the stomach. Doing a little aerobics for the arms. Working the wrists.

"Why?" She's looking at me through her legs, splayed wide.

"I never told you this, but we were pregnant."

"I knew. Frankie."

"Frankie? She told you before I could tell you?"

"It slipped. But she was also surprised you hadn't told me. You had your window. Also what's with this 'we'?" She shifts positions. Arches her back. I roll my wrists. Do my best.

"She was pregnant. But she decided against it. We decided against it. I wasn't fully committed, but then she went through with it."

"Did she clue you in?"

"I mean it wasn't a hundred percent. Taking chops in the on-deck circle."

"What does that mean?"

"I didn't know it was so immediate. Honestly, I figured having a kid would give me a reason to get my shit together. I thought maybe I could talk her out of it." I crack my knuckles, feel the comfort of the little fizz.

"Ricky, there are a hundred stupid reasons to have kids, and that's at the top of the list, right beneath thinking the kid will keep the romance going."

"I want to be a better person, but what do I do when I feel like her choice doesn't sit right with me?"

"Listen, Ricky." Mom stops the vid clip. She squares up and looks me in the eyes. "Do you want me to tell you what you want to hear, or do you want me to tell you to man up and be truthful with her? You'll only grow to resent her if you don't tell her straightaway. I'm not saying end it off the bat, but at least tell her how you feel. Go from there. You know I love the both of you. Just don't rush into a decision. But shoot straight. You owe that to her and to yourself."

I nod, sit silent for a sec while she's winding down. She fast-forwards the clip, because it's too long. She wants to get to the good parts. The lying down and breathing. The yoga teacher on-screen flows in super speed: appendages move like the arms of a clock in a time-travel montage.

"I'm on her side. If she thought you were both in on it, why does it matter that she didn't tell you the exact date and time? She probably did you a favor not dragging you along. Anyway, didn't she kill off a ton of your kids every time she . . ." And she does the universal jerking-hand-and-tongue-in-cheek symbol for giving a blow job. Laughs. This is where I get my sense of humor. She's trying to get me to crack a grin.

"Goddammit, Mom."

"What? Like I never lived? My first name isn't 'Mom.'"

"Times like this I wish Dad was here."

"Why do you have to bring up the Patron Saint of Skipping Town? Feel like he would take your side? Because you're both men? Or because you're a couple of dipshits?" She's lying down now. Her body prone while she's giving me a verbal lashing.

"Neither answer leaves me looking good."

"You're goddamn right, now stop getting my blood pressure up. I'm in Shavasana."

She salutes the sun or something. I wipe my hands on my extra-stretchy-waistband sweatpants. Waddle away, because my legs fell asleep.

CHAPTER EIGHT

WE'RE AT YARDBIRDS, smoking cigs on the outside benches. "We" meaning Frankie and me. Humid, armpits-drenched-in-sweat night. Even if degrees don't reach triple digits, it still feels like walking through soup. Nighttime barely brings relief. It's still thick, sun or no sun. Even the bugs zig lazily.

Yardbirds is the best dive bar in Omaha. It's the easy bet. Yardbirds or Schrempf's, but Schrempf's was bought out by a big-name Omaha band a few years back and they installed a beer garden and a tiki bar in the back room, so it suddenly feels like something you'd find in Austin, Texas, or some equally try-hard, claims-its-weirdness-on-a-bumper-sticker city. Yardbirds is dark wood. Yardbirds is a punk-rock jukebox. Yardbirds is cash-only.

Frankie glimmers under the neon beer signs. We hold hands in a loose way. She hates sweaty palms, that grade-school full-hand clasp, more she digs the finger interlocked with fingers, fingers fingering other fingers in a sly reminder that we're here together, but also, on some level, a nod at fucking. She runs her hand loosely across my shoulders, gently sweeps my scaffolded neck. "Poor baby," she says. "You look like a sad dog." She scratches behind my ear.

"Lower, actually," I say, serious about an itch that's been plaguing me. One of those phantom yearnings where you scratch at the general region and it turns out it's a whole other body part away. Weird brain tricks. Frankie gets at it for me. I can't even sit straight up right now, because it feels like my spine is humming.

"This okay?" I ask, and lie down, my head across her lap, facing up at her. The rest of my body stretched out on the bench.

"Sure, babe."

I need to broach the big deal. Need to point out the elephant in the room. Shoot it in its fat, tusked face. But I also have to go about this with a sense of delicacy. Have to be honest, but not harsh. Ease into it.

"You killed our kid," I say instead.

"What?" she says sleepily. Like she didn't hear me or didn't believe what I said.

I'm sure she heard me. She ashes her cigarette, gives me a look like she's waiting for my next move. I keep my eyes on her tiny fire.

"Frankie, baby, I love you. I do."

"But? What's coming next?"

"What do you mean what's coming next?"

"It's like when people say, 'I'm not racist, but . . .' There's always a 'but.'"

"But every time I look at you: watching Netflix, brushing your teeth, rifling through your closet to find your work shirt, I see what could've been. It's like I see us and then I see the future us. Gray hairs, but still cool. We've got two daughters. They're your spitting image. One has my nose."

"So, even in this made-up future for us, this is way off, like we're old folks. How many years down the line?" She ticks numbers off on her fingers. Decades per digit. "Ten? Twenty years down the line? Even your dreams are more pragmatic than you. We couldn't have done it now. Don't you get that?" Her voice rises in pitch.

"Yeah," I say, having to sit up for the seriousness of the occasion. Also because she's ashing on my face, accidentally or not.

Two drunk guys dressed in denim duds and brown Carhartt jackets stumble out of the bar, their arms slung around each other's shoulders. One asks to bum a smoke. I oblige. Frankie says nothing the whole time and stares off. Never found out what the store across the street pushes, but all I know is that they have multicolored Christmas lights up year-round. Next to it is an old-fashioned barber shop. Next to a blood bank.

I know what I have to say next, but I waver. No going back. "But the problem is there's always going to be this thing hanging over us. This life we ended because we weren't ready and we fucked up and got pregnant. I know, I know. Bundle of nerves versus a life. But can't there be a difference between understanding something in your brain and then giving ground on that when your head and your heart go in different directions?"

"Okay, okay, I get that. I'm glad you're being honest, but you've also got to understand every dumbass caves when hypothetical situations meet real life. But it's just like Lena says, 'You shout the slogan, you've got to toe the line.'" Power move. Quoting my mom at me. She looks at me, taps the end of her cigarette, and then brushes the ash off her pants as a thing to do with her hands.

"I don't know if I can," I say. I shrug because I don't know what else to do.

"So what are you saying? You can't move past this?"

I already know the answer, but it sticks in my throat. It's not so much saying it that pauses me, but knowing there's going to be a "before this" and an "after this" halts the next three words like there's a small family of fowl walking across their path.

"I don't know."

"What do you mean you don't know? That requires a pretty yes-or-no answer."

"No. I don't think so."

Frankie stands. She bites her lower lip. It quivers. Her eyes get that filmy look. She's on the verge. "Fuck you," she says, and walks off. I swear it's going to be the last time I see her.

"Wait," I say. She pauses, returns in a slow shuffle, unsure of my next move, and I want to say *Me too*. She almost shivers, but it's deadass hot outside.

"I knew something was wrong."

"Why do you say that?"

"Because I had an abortion, our abortion, and you haven't said anything to me about it. You didn't even ask how I was doing."

"I'm sorry."

"Also, your mom texted me a bunch of weird emojis. Like *Heads up* or *Keep your eyes out*. Like a secret message, but they were almost sexual in nature."

"Look, babe, I want us. I just need time. To think through this."

"Think through this? You're the one who started the way you did. We're not doing this right now. I'm not going to wait around while you hem and haw about whether or not you want us to be a thing. You're going to get your shit together and I'm going home." She throws the finished cig at my feet.

"What? What does that mean?" I ask, but she's already walking away. I'm stunned, so it takes me a sec to realize what just happened. "Come back!" I say, but she's power walking, so she's beyond whistling distance. I hear the sound of pool balls being racked behind the glass. A beater with a spiderwebbed windshield idles outside of Yardbirds, feet from me. The windows are too tinted, so I can't make out the driver. All I hear is the steady hum of the engine.

"Can I help you?" I finally ask.

I hope the window rolls down and a blow-dart gun or pistol with a thick-barreled silencer pokes out of the minor gap and puts me out of my misery. Body slumps, head hits the ashtray. A spray of red across the sidewalk. But the car just putters off. They've had their fill of the shit show.

I go home. Lie in bed chewing on whether or not I made the right move. Grab one of my five pillows and scream into it, slam the back of my head against the headboard. Feel the snap of pain work through my entire body. Did I say the right things? Play them back, but probably a more composed version of me. A me with a monocle saying everything slick and letting her down gently as a kid placing a chick into a bed of hay. I barely get out of bed until she texts me two days later.

She wants to meet at her favorite sushi restaurant, Miso Hungry. It's in North Benson, off the main drag of Dodge. Neighbors a Black beauty supply store and a vape store. Frankie loves these one-of-one, named-after-a-bad-pun places. The owners are actually Japanese, but they moved into what was once a Mexican taqueria and barely updated the decor, so there are Mexican flags and Día de los Muertos sugar skulls everywhere. We'd eat here once a month.

We drive separately because she's getting off work and I'm busy helping Mom figure out the feng shui of a room. When I arrive, it's mostly empty inside as it's past lunch rush, but not quite dinner hours. Frankie is already seated; she's in the same booth we always sit in, posed in the same way I've seen her sitting a hundred times before, one leg crossed over the other at the knees, her one hand holding her phone and the other one free to swipe and scan with the grand gestures of an old-timey baroness. She stands to greet me, and we weirdly hug like two old friends who haven't seen each other in years. She still doesn't know quite how to hug around the collar. She goes in too wide and barely brings her arms around. Or maybe that's as close as she wants to get. She's already ordered Godzilla rolls and deep-fried chicken skins covered in a spicy red sauce. She pushes them to the middle of the table when I sit.

"Next weekend Paloma and Thoreau are coming into town," she says, picking up a chicken skin with her chopsticks. She's skilled at using them. I mostly poke and mangle.

"What?"

"I said Paloma and Thoreau are coming into town—remember them? My Milwaukee friends?"

"No, I remember. Great. But. Next weekend?"

"Yeah? The Friday after this Friday."

"But I thought we were going to talk about—about us. You were there, right?" I try to grip a piece of pink ginger with my chopsticks, but I never could get the mechanics without looking like a child, so I skewer it with one chopstick and pop it into my mouth.

"You're wearing jeans. Must be a formal occasion."

"You know my thighs touch in all my other pants."

"Did you not catch the end that night, or did you black that out?"

"I remember."

"So you really want to do this?"

"I thought we were here to talk about it," I say, then line up my chopsticks and set them down.

"Fill me in."

"I need some time. Or, I don't know, not time. Like I want to talk this through."

"Okay, Ricky, I'm trying to be understanding, but remember you blindsided me outside of Yardbirds. Also, we had plenty of time to talk about this before I went through with it. Where was this gusto then?" Frankie mixes wasabi in with her soy sauce using her chopsticks. When she's done, she licks the tips and gives a wince.

"I admit I should've been up front. I was never fully comfortable with the idea. Yeah, I wanted the kid. And I should've told you. I just thought maybe I could talk you into it. And I knew you were set in your decision, but then you went through with it so suddenly. I'm still pretty fucked-up from my neck thing and no more wrestling, and then this."

"Ricky, I did it precisely because of your injury. I did it for you. For me. For us. Think about your hospital bills. And needing time to take care of yourself. You already knew how I was feeling. I only accelerated the process because it made sense."

"Part of why I didn't want to say anything was because I felt like no matter my opinion, it's your body. Like yeah, I could voice a concern or whatever, but ultimately you'd have that tiny body inside you. But you're right, I should've spoken up."

"Your timing is perfect," Frankie says, rests her chin in her palm, drums her fingers on her cheek.

"Sorry. I'm a fucking idiot."

"Don't say that. That's too easy. Don't give yourself that out. So tell me, where do we go from here?" I fidget with my poke sticks, and we look each other in the eyes.

"I mean, you're saying that like it's a choice."

"It is."

"It doesn't feel like it."

"Don't be ridiculous, Ricky. Put on your big-boy pants. Make a decision and live with it."

"Okay, well, if I'm put on the spot—"

"On the spot?" Frankie says, like she's responding to someone swearing the earth is flat.

"I don't know if I can do this." I look around to make sure we're not being too loud. Make sure no one is eavesdropping. Can't face the busboy if this all goes south. He knows us by our first names.

"Really. You want to throw it all away. We've been through so much, baby. So much. And you want to throw it away?"

"But you threw away our baby." I don't even know why I say it. It's knee-jerk, but also I'm trying to work this out in real time and it's coming out awkward; it's that thing where when you fuck up you want grace from a loved one while possibly fucking up that same loved one. My doubt is killing her spirit.

We both stop. She's not making eye contact. Then she is.

She throws the sushi at me.

Ever open a packet of salty-ass soy sauce and a drip spills? Remember the stink? Imagine getting splashed with a faceful. Getting it all over your shoes and shirt, no service. Frankie storms out. Nearby, a young Hispanic kid is sweeping. He moves the chairs around a table, and the wood-on-wood drag sounds like a surprised bison.

"I'll see you next week with your friends Party and Tabletop," I say to her dust. Fuck. I'm an idiot.

A week later, I'm confused about whether I can even contact her. Due to algorithmic magic, her IG stories present themselves in my feed front and center. Block? Delete? Soft block? Do I care what she thinks? I need a few things back from her. A pillow. Two pairs of sweatpants. Five or so T-shirts, including one of my favorites, a black tee with a giant superimposed Ric Flair face going woo! An old Ak-Sar-Ben racetrack hat that was a gift from Mom. But I'm also afraid that if we do more face time, it'll only drag things out. Better not to pick at the wound.

I text her: *hey, can we talk?*

Frankie: *no*

plz?

y? so you can say more demeaning shit to me?
i'm sorry but you wanted me to be honest
honest & cruel aren't the same thing
fuck so what now

Then an hour and a half of radio silence. I'm too afraid to double text. But then I have to risk a quick question.

hate to ask but can i at least get my stuff back?
fuck you
can you at least donate it?
you want me to pack this stuff up and lug it down there? you going to pay me for the gas?

Thirty minutes later, I get a direct message on Instagram. It's a video clip.

She's wearing my Ric Flair shirt. Out of nowhere, she tears the shirt down the middle, Hogan-style. She's got a bra on underneath, but the ripped shirt almost reveals too much. The whole message is an affront to me. Then she looks in the camera and says, "Fuck your Hulk Hogan shirt."

I'm not sure what's worse: the fact that she acted in this personal attack, a tiny drama for an audience of me . . . Or the fact that she called the Nature Boy "Hogan."

Two months later, it's late at night and I Google her. Her social media presence is minimal. All her accounts are marked private. She's blocked me on every platform. I have to go in anonymous. Free of being me. Still, the details are blocked from prying eyes. At most there's her name. A job title. A handful of public pics. In one of them, she's smiling. Another is her from the back, looking into a gap in the Badlands. Looks like she's got a new gig working at an optometrist, only answering phones for now, but she looks happier and is probably making more consistent money. No word on school. Her relationship status says single, but the same man is beside her in nearly every pic. Looks like he's a Jewish kid pretending at being urban: a twisty hairdo he borrowed from a magazine, a scuffed leather jacket with a high collar, boxy Doc Martens, a tattoo of the word "Bang" on his pointer finger. Profile say his name's Eamon. Bet he's soft as mayonnaise. His teeth give him away; they're too straight. Nothing a good dropkick couldn't fix.

CHAPTER NINE

I PAY PILGRIM a visit. Well, Pilgrim and the other kids, but especially Pilgrim. My right-hand man. My bud.

I sign in at the front desk. Pocket the pen. Make small talk with the office staff. Principal McWhorter is out. I give Marjorie the reason for my official visit. Marjorie is the office receptionist, who recently got a blunt-cut bob, which, no knock on Marjorie, doesn't seem like the haircut for someone named Marjorie; better fits an art gallerist with too many scarves. But go Marge. I tell Blunt-Cut Marge that I'm here to see the Intertribal Council.

"Ricky, I think—"

"I'd like to speak to your manager," I say, in a nod to her haircut, and while she looks confused, I try to leave quickly, but I'm about as stiff as a robot butler. Although I have a whole door, desk, and bank of phones between us, so I make the slip. Marge doesn't try to take chase. She calls after me as I walk down the hallways. See posters for rallies. After-school clubs. Government body. Most of the school has emptied out. A couple of kids play intramural basketball in one of the gyms.

Group of girls re-create K-pop choreo in an empty room. I make my way to the second floor, notice the lights out.

Nobody is there. Did they switch rooms? Is that what Marjorie was trying to tell me?

I have to double back to Marjorie's desk. "Sorry, Marjorie," I say, give her back her pen. "Nice haircut, by the way."

"I was going to tell you they're done for the semester," she says.

"No Pilgrim?"

"Who?"

I forgot what time of the year it is. The end of the semester already came, and I have no way of saying good-bye to Pilgrim or any of the other seniors. It's not like I have their numbers. At best, I can hope that one of the returning students will still be in contact with them next semester. Pass on a message.

I really wanted to talk to my bud, too. Most of my life has been Mom and me. I had a few friends in high school. But no lifelong bonds. Yuri, my childhood pal. Johnny, before the betrayal. Didn't even have enough contenders to have a clique. I mostly ran solo. A lot of that is from growing up dirt-poor with a single mom: that us-against-the-world mentality. And then when I got old enough to wrestle, I traveled a lot. Which meant missed dates and celebrations, meals in empty motel rooms of single-serving-size snacks chilling in a sink full of hallway cooler ice.

Pilgrim is like a younger brother to me. Going to miss our chats. I never told him this, but I once had a dream where he was regular, adult-size him cradling baby-size me, and I kept smushing his chubby cheeks together. Not sure what it meant, but it was adorable.

Reality is, unless I run into him randomly in, like, a Walmart aisle, I'll likely never see him again. Could probably stalk his ass on Instagram. Or Twitter. Pull an older-folks move and add him on Facebook. But maybe it's better this way: a clean break.

I remember when I knew I'd won his trust. A month after I'd arrived.

The council had just lost their chaperone. Every club had to have a teacher represent them. And their last rep just transferred to a school in Millard. Big money. McDonald's and Runza in the commons. So Pilgrim and the rest of the council were stressed for representation. Brainstormed backup plans. When they showed up to the next meeting, in the teacher's seat sat a life-size man made out of duct tape. Took me at least three hours. Figured they could pull some sleight of hand. Throw clothes on him, wheel him around, and if anyone passed by at a distance they'd mistake him for a flesh-and-blood instructor. Buy them some time. Hijinks is what high school is all about. Only life isn't like a movie, and the other custodians had to trash him almost immediately, but they had my back and blamed a student, so it didn't look like I was wasting school materials. End of the day, the kids knew.

They appreciated me going out on a limb. It made them laugh, too.

"Nice gesture," Pilgrim said. Tara asked me if I could make her a duct-tape wallet. Even Grey Cloud seemed impressed.

Wrestling doesn't really have any retirement ceremonies. At best, a wrestler might go out in a blaze of a match. But there isn't an actual act to signal the good-bye other than an announcement on the mic. In MMA, when a fighter is done, he or she might take off their gloves and set them in the center of the ring. I know I left a note, but I want to do something more. I sneak down to the custodial closets. Find a roll of duct tape. Maybe I should leave the whole thing. Or fashion a quick mini-figure. That might be more obvious than a random duct-tape roll. As I palm the roll, I hear a door open behind me. It's Sweet Lew. We call him that because he loves Pearl Jam. Sweet Lew works with me on the custodial staff. He and I aren't super close, but we're cordial. He's an older gentleman who keeps to himself; has such incredible posture, I swear he sleeps in a coffin.

"Things that bad, Ricky?" Sweet Lew asks, sees me holding the tape. He ambles over, pulls out his wallet, slides out a ten-spot, and then tucks it into my breast pocket. Taps my chest with the flat of his hand. Turns around and walks away.

Truth be told, I could use both the cash and the roll. Could keep both and walk out. I have a flash of an idea to leave a reminder for Tara. She'll pass it on. I try to finesse out a wallet. Can't be that hard. It's like an open envelope. Some folds. A few creases. I wing it. After about ten minutes I realize that I end up with something folded like one of those paper boats you make as a child, and the capper is that I've also accidentally taped the ten-dollar bill inside. I leave the whole thing inside a desk they'll have to access whenever they return; I pray they figure it out. Godspeed, Tara, you elbow-pierced genius. Godspeed.

CHAPTER TEN

MY DOC'S OFFICE is in a strip mall. The signage is an eyesore. Three fonts for one name. Probably the doc's college kid majoring in graphic design did it. The practice is next to a fast-casual bánh mì place and a shoe store. Years ago, I went to the shoe store and tried on three different pairs of sneakers. I kept saying, "Really need to test them," and would quick pivot, making the sneakers squeak on the faux-hardwood floor. And then I'd do high knees for a minute straight. "Testing," I'd say. Didn't make the purchase. Never been back.

Doc Hairdo is what I call my doctor. He's a damn handsome man, very cultivated. He doesn't have a chin or a bod; he's a squat Irish guy who barely clears five seven, but his hair really brings the room to a standstill. Regal in its swoop and bounce. Gets some real altitude.

He also has piercing green eyes. Mom says she doesn't think he's handsome. She says his face is too flat, which sounds like something Donnie would say, but I know she's just not into doctors. Mom goes for plumbers or welders. She's always been averse to dating anyone making real money. Thinks it invites insincerity.

"Checking up," he says. "Any pain? Discomfort?" He's tapping at a chart. Puts the pen in his mouth. Decidedly non-doc tics.

Things are progressing at the rate he thinks they should be.

"Which means what?" I ask.

"Wait and see," he says.

Doc Hairdo hands me a pamphlet. It has a URL and a QR code on it.

"You can't just text this to me?"

"You don't need my personal number."

"Not *you*, you."

He taps the pamphlet with the mouthed pen. It leaves a wet spot.

Later, I type the address into my phone's browser. Fuck QR codes. It's a list of general advice on how to pass the time postsurgery. A computer could've cobbled better hacks. Do a crossword puzzle, discover new music, learn a card trick. Two odd ones: Read the entirety of Harry Potter and learn the lost art of lace-making. Not sure what spinster freelancer cobbled together this mess, but I saw the movie based on one of those books and all I remember was a poor nerd waving a stick with his nerd friends. Also, I don't know when's the last time I even fingered lace in the wild.

My takeaway: I need new hobbies. Expose myself to the bigger world. Kill hours and build brain cells besides watching Netflix recs. Algorithm is all off anyway, pushing Japanese anime or British bake-offs, because I use the account of a kid who once sold me a fifth but didn't have change and split the difference with his mom's access.

CHAPTER ELEVEN

AND THEN I see Bojorquez. Or, rather, he sees me. I'm shopping for groceries at that filthy No Frills on Saddle Creek. The parking lot is all cracked plots and crack pipes and sniff vials. Inside is all age-spotted old folks with hairy moles palming fruit or Hessians in ripped-sleeve metal T-shirts shopping for cheap hooch. I'm throwing groceries in my cart I know I can't afford. Hoping my debit card can cover the goods. Bojorquez catches me in the parking lot. He's sitting in a big, souped-up truck. It's got the candy-colored paint of a grape Jolly Rancher. It's also got those balls dangling from the back, and he's got the words Tahoe transfigured to say My Hoe. Class act. I'm surprised he recognizes me. I'm at least twenty-five pounds heavier. I've got a scuzzy beard that's more patchwork than complete set, and underneath my coat my sweat suit is grimed in the salt rind of everyday sweat. I don't look like a functioning human being. I look like a message board troll who hurtles words like "soy boy" against anyone who dares whisper the word "diversity."

"Twohatchet! Ricky! Ricky!" Bojorquez calls my name. He could sweet-talk a grandma into forking over a pension check. Bojorquez looks healthy. Gives off the glow of money. Of success. Of fucking well. He looks strong as ever, but a bit leaner.

"Vegan," he says to me, as if reading my mind. "I'm vegan now. No meat." He pats at his hardened stomach. Also his voice is off, accent gone.

We're in the parking lot, and I'm toeing a near-dead patch of grass that broke through the concrete, holding my barely groceries. When I went to tally everything, I didn't even have enough for half. I had to play dumb and slide the remaining groceries into the "to be returned" baskets. I left with a plastic bag of potato chips, toothpaste, and a six-pack of Smartwater.

"How've you been, Ricky?" Bojorquez asks. He's leaning out of the driver's-side window smoking a black cigarette. Something European. He's got a gold ring on his pinkie that's a lion's head. He beckons me to get in. I have to cross to the other side, step to the passenger door, sidle up, slide in, leave the door ajar so the overhead light glows our faces, shows our hands.

"You look like you've woken up on the wrong side of the bed."

"Yeah, neck is still sore. Still in this thing for another few months."

"For what it's worth, I didn't think America should have taken you out."

"So whose idea was it, then? Donnie? Was it Donnie?"

"No, it was America."

I notice a bag of apples at my feet. Fuji would be my best guess, but I don't know an apple from an apple. A few stray cores litter the floor. "Still eating apples?" I ask. Far as small talk has ever gone in the annals of small talk, this is my worst work. Bojorquez knows it; I know it.

"Also, I gotta say something," I say. Then I say something. "What the hell is up with your voice?"

"C'mon, Ricky."

"What?"

"It's all part of the show."

"Part of what?"

"Even this truck is an act. It's my brother-in-law's. I drive it around to events, but normally I'm in a Ford Fiesta."

"Wait. What?" I scratch at my beard and hope the flakes are from yesterday's potato chips.

"You're not that dense. We all do it. I do it. You definitely do it."

"Do what?"

"The tomahawks. The hair dye. The leather fringe. They eat it up."

"Why did you always talk like that, then? Even backstage?" I feel sweat secreting from between my thighs, from my general ass area. Heated leather seats.

"I'm method, I guess. Never wanted anyone to catch me speaking the Queen's English."

"My mind is blown right now. Facundo, too?"

"Well, he definitely has an accent, but Facundo just did it because he was helping me. Man, I'll tell you the one hundred percent no-bullshit truth of it. I don't even really like wrestling. Well, not at first. But it was my younger brother's dream. And he passed early, a few years ago. So I gave it a shot. I was always the better athlete. Played Division II football. But once I took to it, I kept going."

"Sorry to hear about your brother," I say.

"Died serving overseas. It's been almost ten years now."

"What's Facundo doing?"

"Back in Mexico. Facundo has an engineering degree. He'll be better off than all of us." Bojorquez looks at his face in the rearview mirror; I'm still in shock and awe. We make eye contact in the mirror. "Do me a favor, though: Don't say anything. To them, I'm the bad guy. They love me, but I'm the bad guy."

Bojorquez isn't wrong. Wrestling is this broken snow globe separate from everything else. It's as if every hard-fought inch in the real world of people trying to push back from the edges hasn't happened. Or is

back to mid-nineties levels of dimwit bliss. Part of it is how we, the
wrestlers, play up our gimmicks. Only a few of us can pivot like Hunter
Hearst Helmsley into Triple H into The Game. Or Stone Cold previously
being The Ringmaster. You may not get that second chance. And we
don't have a team of writers like in the bigs, the WWE. So those of us
who already have a built-in angle will often lean in. Because also, not
that this is an excuse, but our audience isn't exactly full of PhDs who
would point out the flaws in our racial representation. Our fans love
that broad-strokes bullshit and we feed it to them. Does that make us
part of the problem? Yes. But we still need to take a paycheck. It's like
starving actors who take stupid stereotypical roles: math whiz, virgin
nerd, gangbanger. Fuck. Now I'm thinking about my involvement and
feeling the bubble guts of guilt. Thanks, Bojorquez, you fucking ethics
professor. Way to make me muse.

We have little to talk about after that. I fake a thing I have to be
getting to. I utter the word "portfolio." I leave Bojorquez's truck. He
signals at me with his fat ring shining. I duck my head back into the
cab, but at a weird angle, only bending at the waist due to my current
state. Bojorquez slips his hand into my cervical collar. I can feel a bunch
of bills folded over on themselves. It's substantial. I don't want to take
it out and count it in front of him. It'd feel disrespectful. But I'm also
not sure why he didn't slip it into my coat pocket. Like he's trying to be
playful, but I also now have a bunch of flapping bills tickling my chin.

Instead I step outside and watch as he watches me. I walk a few
feet away and as he makes eye contact, I jokingly shoot him the double
birds, middle fingers, say, "*Adiós, muchacho.*" It's a thing he did in the
ring. He smiles.

After I get home, I pull out the fat stack. Not like rapper fat. But it's
a lot right now. And it's more than he had to give me, which was zip.
I'm not sure I would've done it had I been in his position. I want to say
thanks, but am not sure how.

I find this old GoPro that I once bought because I was really into BMX biking for a few weeks. Wanted to film my stunts.

I pull out a few of the small bills. Burn the money with the end of a joint. Record a diatribe about not being for sale. About how Bojorquez is a sellout who tried to bribe me. His win was a dirty win. He bought off the higher-ups, I allege. I may have said "dirty," and I may have said "Mexican," but I didn't say them in tandem, so there's that. I upload the video as a response to the latest Pro Mag YouTube video.

I glance at the video once, a week after the fact. View count is in the dozens. As many comments. I never read one. In my mind, they're all wildly applauding my verve. I imagine they'll only multiply. World-wide meltdowns where my fans come out of the woodwork, screaming obscenities of agreement at their monitors. Putting back-alley favela hexes in goat's blood on Bojorquez in Brazil. Burning effigies of him dipped in vodka in my honor in Russia. Cheering my genius in Japanese. I hope he gets the message.

CHAPTER TWELVE

AFTER I BURN the money and post the video, I get a text from Frankie: *god you're your biggest hero.* Nothing like an out-of-the-blue text from an ex to say, *hey, dummy.*

I text back: *new phone, who dis?* Admittedly, I'm high. Another few pulls from the vape. Another handful of poppers. *the god i pray to has a better beard*

She doesn't text back.

I scarf Vics they gave me for my neck and stay up all night bouncing from a shiny high to wincing through the aches and pains up and down my spine. I down the pills with a few beers. Nothing crazy, but a six-pack to dull things out.

I wake up the next morning and know that I have little left. Less than lint's inside-out pockets.

No job, no girl, no kid. I run in place to burn the hurt out. I run until my calves pulse and my shins feel like they'll split in half. Okay, "running" is putting a spin on it. Light jogging. But I have the stamina of a tiny child with rickets at this point, although their slow is due to weak bones and bowlegs. Mine's more soft gut and stiff neck. I have to run in a way that keeps my upper half steady. I look like an alien who read a book about running.

After ten minutes, I know it's a bad idea, because everything aches, from the soles of my feet to the top of my head. My hair hurts.

Growing up, instead of dealing with deep-seated feels, I'd work it out, like in an actual workout. I'd go so hard that sweat would pour off me and I'd pretend that every drop was my real problem wicking away from me.

Any decent shrink would point to this being at the root of my fascination with wrestling.

Wrestling being a stand-in for no dad. I mean, he existed. He was out there somewhere, but he wasn't here. My dear mother, Arlene Powell, told me she met a tall, dark, sharp-jawed Native dude at a powwow in Lawrence, Kansas. They ate Native tacos. Talked Rock Chalk basketball. He was a student at Haskell. She was a journalism major at KU. They saw each other for five or six months, and then he abruptly called it off. Then he came back, and they ran hot and cold. Until the last time. She was late approximately three weeks later and went to a drugstore off Wakarusa. She bought three different brands of pregnancy tests while getting side-eyed from the Midwestern, middle-aged cashier with a bob and zero accent, her voice flatter than Kansas, and she put her hand over my mom's hand and told her, "Honey, there's always prayer." Mom went straight to her dorm and had to pee on a stick in her shared bathroom. Watched and waited. Wiped off the pee she got on her hands. When she told my dad, it was over coffee at a diner. She said he said all the right things: "I'll do my best by you." "If you want to go through with it, I'll support you one hundred percent." He ate a cruller; she didn't have an appetite. After a day or two, she went to visit him at his apartment and his roommates, two long-haired Phishheads, told her he'd moved.

Grabbed a trash bag full of his stuff and fled. Told them he'd figure out the logistics of transferring later, just needed air. She never saw him again. Only remembered his name and a few details.

Minus the major blunder of skipping town, which she definitely held against him, she mostly talked about him in gentle terms with the occasional needle of a loved one. I don't think she ever stopped loving him. From what I gleaned from stories, their entire relationship was only really on for about six months and then extended on and off for another five at most. It was around a year of her life, but something about the relationship, although she'd had plenty afterward, stuck to her ribs like molasses.

She only clued me in on who he actually was when I was about five years old. Prior to that, when I asked who my dad was, she'd tell me "that man," and point to a wrestler on TV, an action hero in a movie, a firefighter in a commercial. She told me Dad had to go bye-bye, but he loved me very much. I took it at face value and continued playing with my Ninja Turtles, zoomed my Hot Wheels. When I got older, I did feel the emptiness of a lack of dad, and I did a little research into Native Americans. One summer I watched *The Last of the Mohicans* seventeen times. That was about as far as I took it. But not Mom. She always had a soft spot. Though not a strong enough yearning that she felt the need to find him.

This was years before Google. Before Al Gore even had the fever dream of the Internet. She couldn't afford to hire a private eye, some gumshoe to track down her baby's dad. Mom was also a firebrand, a full-fledged feminist in the days they weren't afraid to use the F-word, and figured if any man was going to cut ties and run, then she didn't need him in her life anyway. She told me once there are only two things you need to wrangle and break in this life, and a man isn't one of them.

I once asked her, recently, if she'd ever been tempted to look him up. Find him, now that the finding's easier. She said no. She said, "If I saw a photo of him vacationing with his family in Barbados or flipping burgers on a grill with a Kiss the Cook apron on, I couldn't bear to stand it. I'd probably find out where he lived, grab my .38, drive down to his home, and point the barrel at his smug face. I'd pull the trigger, knowing it was empty, just to see him squirm." People laughed at that lady astronaut who wore a diaper and drove cross-country to stake her claim in a love triangle. But a heart will pump dumb on love.

Mom was dad, mom, boss, you name it, all wrapped up in five feet, four inches of no give.

Mom is tops, but somewhere deep inside me, buried so damn deep you'd need radar to find your way, is still that tickle of not knowing. Measurements. Hat size. Aftershave brand. And the even more important shit: political positions, family health history, favorite football team.

She never truly disparaged him in front of me. When I was younger, she talked about him being away like he was on a long work trip. When I got older and she explained what it meant for him not to be part of our lives, I got little snippets about him. Stories. A candid picture. He was quiet; a brooder. But if you were trusted to his inner circle, he really opened up. Was witty. Loved to crack wise. Gave everyone nicknames. Didn't play sports, but was naturally athletic. They went to a friend's backyard party, where a tournament ensued—axe throwing, three-legged races, etc. He crushed the competition.

He's been as real to me as Superman, Hulk Hogan, Mr. T. Kayfabe versus reality. But now missing out on my own kid, and also feeling lost in every goddamned aspect of my life, makes me feel like I need to do something dramatic to jar me back on track.

This sounds fucked-up, but maybe he could help me feel better about not being a dad.

In my weed-and-pill-addled brain, I have this crazy idea that if I find my dad, if I can pick his brain somehow, I can get it right. Whatever "it" is. What decades of feel-good family romps and prime-time television have taught me is a cue-the-sad-tunes moment. In walks Pops to give me a chuck under the chin and sage words. Tosses me the pigskin.

Only I don't own a football, know close to zilch about my dad, where he is, and what he looks like. But even after all these years, I still want to know.

I scour articles with glimpses of similar names. Google Map a path. Omaha to Lawrence, Kansas, and back. Crunch numbers. Three hundred ninety-one miles, round trip. Six hours and eighteen minutes, total. Not counting stops. A skip and a jump.

Two more days pass, blurry. I do more research than I ever did in any Comp Rhet class. Save links. Screenshot docs. Print off what I need and stuff it into an empty folder. Figure if I do go through with it, it'll be easier to read fully printed pages than thumb through my phone on the road.

I fall asleep to an animal flick on Netflix that posits our greatest leap was when we learned to harness fire. Gorillas gnawing on sticks. They say it's what separates us. "I'll be damned," I say, feel the tender give of a puffy Cheeto between my teeth.

When I wake up on day three, I'm in the middle of a nest of mussed sheets and the fallout from the aftermath of seventy-two hours of obsessive Googling. Cheetos, Funyuns, Hostess CupCakes, McDonald's hamburger wrappers, empty 20 oz. bottles of Pepsi and Squirt. Grease stains, orange smears, a smashed chocolate cupcake underneath me. At least I pray that's what that is.

The animal doc asks me if I'm still watching. Yes, I'm still watching. I click play.

Narrator cues in midsentence: ". . . close-knit as it gets." Gray wolves. Alpha dad takes care of the pack. Guards the domain. Brings back regurgitated goodies to the young pups. But also makes time to play, they say. Cut to daddy wolf and baby wolves frollicking. Nipping. "Males and females can form lifelong bonds," the narrator says in a deep British voice. Shows papa wolf giving a deep yawn. Heading back into the den with the fam. Beddy-bye time. Drawl-y flute music plays under the images of the wolves nestling.

Before I pass out, I have a vision: one of those on the edge of slumber mirages. It's Baby Me with Big Pilgrim. The suddenness of it jars me back awake. I'm holding my phone in my hand, and I decide what could a quick search hurt? If you grew up in the past thirty years, you know how to find someone on the Internet. It's a skill you hone. Like previous generations using record players or flirting face-to-face. You can meet a cute stranger at a diner in a middle-of-nowhere mountain town and within minutes find out her favorite movie is *Legally Blonde 2: Red, White & Blonde*.

But for some reason, I can't find Pilgrim. Sure, it's not his real name. But I also can't find him when I know his acquaintances: Tara, Grey Cloud, and the others. Even searching through their friends or followers lists, or at least what I can access, since some info is private, leads to very little. I'm stumped.

I want to add Grey Cloud. Ask him straight-up. My finger hovers over the follow button. I accidentally click it because of my thick-ass sausage fingers and then immediately click unfollow. Fuck. I hope he didn't get that notification. I'm going to have to delete all my social media, quit my job, and change my identity. I throw my phone behind my bed as if that's going to solve anything. I'm just going to have to fish it out tomorrow.

. . .

In the morning, Mom is in the living room surrounded by sixteen beach balls, all with the number 16 squiggly written on them. She's packing and sorting, has incense burning in a ceramic holder she made herself. Room smells like hippie pits.

"Alice from next door just had a beach-themed Sweet Sixteen. Her mom basically gave these to me. Had no use for them after the fact."

"What are you going to do with sixteen beach balls?"

"Use them when Nana celebrates her ninety-first birthday. It's only coming up in thirteen years. The beach balls work for Tampa."

That's Mom. Being a single parent of a growing boy who needed to eat and eat and eat, she had to learn to be thrifty. She's better off financially now, but she still has the same habits. Won't throw out anything from her fridge or pantry unless it gives off a smell. Hasn't thrown out any old clothes since she was in her twenties. Still asks for extra bread to box up at any decent restaurant and still palms sauce packets and tucks them into her purse.

"Listen, Lena," I start, "you're not going to like this."

She sits back, beach ball in her hand like she's about to serve, gives me a hard look. "You're going to find your dad."

"How the fuck did you know?"

"Boy, I've known you since birth. I know every scar and mole. I knew one day you'd bring it up. It was only a matter of time. Also, I found this," she says, and pulls out the folder. "I figured this was either about that or you were finally coming out."

"You thought I was coming out and typed out a speech?"

"Well, you've heard of the words 'hypermasculine' and 'overcompensating.' You've spent a lot of your early twenties surrounded by half-naked men."

"You find a thesaurus recently?"

"Edith sent me an article on Facebook."

"Sent you an article?"

"Linked me, you know."

"You're armchairing me?"

"Baby, this is my new education. I never finished college, and now I got all this at my fingertips. You just want to keep an old woman down."

"What are you talking about?" I gently toss a beach ball into the air. The 16 smears.

"Fuck the patriarchy, baby."

"What's a patriarchy baby?"

CHAPTER THIRTEEN

MOM, IN TYPICAL Mom mode, tries to talk me out of it. Or, rather, she gives me some perspective. But at the last possible second, when she's helping me get my Mustang road-ready. Not sure if this is an insidious Mom move that she's worked out so that she can tick off that box, throw an I-told-you-so at me later.

I drive an Acapulco Blue 1967 Ford Mustang fastback. The gas mileage is terrible, and the back end slides like crazy come Omaha winters. It's a ridiculous car that I only bought because a friend of a friend's grandfather rarely drove it and was looking to get it out of his garage. But of course I bought it, because a Mustang, especially an older Mustang, is like a leather jacket. You convince yourself that it doesn't mean you're trying too hard, that you do look cool, you do look cool, you do look cool.

My favorite part of my car, though, is this diorama I've set up on the dash: a patch of land and a few cows, a barn, and a windmill. The same grandfather who sold me the ride was throwing out pieces of an old miniature railroad set. Reminds me of home no matter what's past the windshield.

"You sure you want to do this?" she asks, standing in the driveway, wiping her hands clean with a rag. I have the know-how, but due to my injury, Mom changes the oil and replaces the wiper fluid. Checks the air on the tires. "What about your neck? It's going to be murder on the body," she says. She starts making sounds and vibrating like when you're cresting on a roller coaster and you feel every bump on your body. Doc did mention not driving, but I figure enough time has passed that hopefully my spine and neck are doing their duty. What the hell else am I supposed to do? Take a train like that magic nerd going to his magic nerd school?

"I'll take as many breaks as I need to. Pull over as much as possible."

"Take this with you," she says, hands me a seat cushion. "You could cradle an egg in there, sit on top of it, and not crack it." She stops. "What if you don't find what you're looking for?"

"Mom, I'm not expecting anything."

"You'll be okay with that? You'll be okay with coming back empty-handed?"

"As long as I know that I tried, I'll be all right."

"Give it a good college try."

"I never finished."

"That's two of us."

Mom bids me good-bye. "Good-bye," she says. She plays a funeral dirge on the old mouth trumpet. Claps me on the shoulder, then she goes in for the full hug. Arms at my waist, hard to breathe. She takes a sniff.

"I'm not dying."

"You never know."

"Jesus, Mom," I say. I can't tell if she's joking. She knows I've essentially lived on the road since my wrestling career took off. But this time is different. She's being unusually tender about my trip. Not sure if it's the neck injury or the dad-seeking that's making her more doting. Either way, she's packed me the cushion, a sandwich, and snacks, and now this big show right before I shove off.

The only thing I have to go on is a name, a story, and a blurry photo. She showed it to me a handful of times when I was younger, when I had questions about who dad was, but then she tucked it away after she walked in on me staring at it too intently one day when I was nine. She felt like I was too invested at such a tenderhearted age in someone I may never meet. But she did tell me the story behind it.

Jeremiah and her had spent all night smoking cigarettes, talking life, and listening to old country records: Patsy Cline, Merle Haggard, Emmylou Harris. At three a.m., they found their way to an all-night diner. A diner that's no longer open in Lawrence, having long been filled by a cupcake bakery. They were still young, wide-eyed to the world. Right at that age where possibility seemed just at their fingertips. She was a junior in college, and he was enrolled at Haskell.

In the pic he's wearing a navy-blue denim jacket and his hair is long, ratty. But he's still handsome and lean. Looks like he was carved from a hard metal. She's to his right. She's also wearing denim, a fringed jacket over a white tee that says TIGHT and features a cartoon cat squeezed into a telephone booth. The letters are in this nineties neon font: all swoops and curls like it was hastily handwritten with a highlighter. She's smiling at him, because he just said something funny. He's looking straight at the camera. That was their last good night together. She's kept the Polaroid for over twenty years.

When I ask her to dig it out, she finds it slipped between the pages of a book. *Sex and Rage* by Eve Babitz. An old edition. Except the photo is nothing like she remembers. And somehow I forgot, too. My memory warped to her retelling. The actual one is hard to make out in one corner because age or oxidation has yellowed it intensely. And in it she's not laughing at all. And she's not staring at him; they're both staring off into the distance. Clinton-era *American Gothic*. It looks late at night, but they're not in a diner, they're in a Laundromat. The detergent dispenser is visible in the left corner. Old boxes of Tide, Oxydol, Surf.

"Oh, that's right," she tells me, touches her hand to the yellow corner. "I burned all the good ones."

I toss a backpack full of clothes and an old laptop into the passenger seat and get ready to leave for Lawrence. I start driving and see Mom posing as a T. rex in the rearview, something she used to do for me when I was a kid waiting for her to come back to the car after she'd gone to run an errand. Closer than they appear, but scary close already. Before I'm even that far from the driveway, she's already turning back in. Great, I think. Then, when I'm no less than five minutes away, as I'm about to pull onto the interstate, she calls me. I almost don't answer.

"Ricky!" she says. "Come back. You left something important."

I cut a U-turn; zoom back in half the time. Gun the gas. Almost flatten an indecisive squirrel.

"What is it?" I ask, rolling down my window as I pull back into the driveway.

"I'm driving," she says, waiting, a duffel bag already packed.

Mom is as strong-headed as they come.

"We both knew this was going to happen," she says, yips it up.

She's got an oversized straw cowboy hat on and a smile so wide I notice her gum disease.

CHAPTER FOURTEEN

LAWRENCE IS MOM'S old stomping grounds. When she was a young undergrad heat-seeking the fellow hard bods to suck face and procreate. No judgment here. She was a pretty young thing with a name like Lena and a beauty mark Marilyn-style, and she had long, straight blonde hair that she hadn't cut but to freshen the edges in over seven years. She was dream-girl material for many a postpubescent Jayhawk.

Lawrence now is clean-cut. Rebuilt. Mom says in the old days you couldn't walk a block without running into a panhandler. So many cities would force them out. Pass bills, slap cuffs. Lawrence used to be more lax about lingerers. Now, you can't spot a single one on the strip. Old buildings were refurbished into boutiques, pubs, and breweries or faux-hip chain stores pushing homogenized independence. The tear in a pair of hundred-and-fifty-dollar jeans represents freedom from the tyranny of man's denim oppression. Or at least that's what the tag reads.

I'm not even sure there is much to go on in Lawrence, but I have a hunch someone might still remember an old Native hanging around.

I wonder what he looks like now. Did he age gracefully? Grow stoic and chiseled, wear bandanas and turquoise? Maybe he returned, made something of himself. Owns a small business off the main strip. Sells handmade whittled-wood signs to townies. Or, more than likely, he's long gone. Left hints of a past life, like an old bar tab, a tarnished rep— faded memories, but nothing of substance. No hard evidence. Ghosts can't leave thumbprints.

We go to his last listed apartment under the ruse of wanting to rent it to get ahold of the landlord. Calling it a shithole would be generous. Dilapidated wood slapped with a weird shade of puke green that has gone even paler under at least four decades of Kansas sun. Looks like the landlord lives above the listing. In the parking lot, we ask a man and a woman dressed in matching sweatpants and they point over to the blue-green pool. A gangly-ass man lies on an outdoor chaise lounge poolside, the lean of his body giving off the vibe he's had a few too many. Also the crumpled-up Lime-A-Ritas at his feet. Dude has a droopy pompadour and bad acne scars that pock up his entire face, and he's shirtless, holding a neon-green plastic water pistol. He keeps twirling it on his pointer finger, gunslinger-style. Says his name is Levi.

Levi says, "Last of the Mohicans I remember was a dude named Jeremy. That was a long time ago, though."

"Jeremiah?" Mom asks, stands at a distance. She's not afraid, but she knows something about him is off.

"Sorry, last what?" I ask. I try not to show my anger, but I have a resting fuck-you face that rivals any middle-aged mom waiting a minute too long for her Starbucks order.

"What you gettin' in a huff for? You halfie?"

"I swear—"

"Now, now, how was I to know? You look white as a president." Levi twirls his gun once more, puts it up to his lips, pulls the trigger. "Didn't mean to offend. It's the gin." He cocks the gun at us. "Listen, I'll tell you I do remember he had a forwarding address."

"Probably his mom's place," Mom says. Mom and I look at each other. We start to walk off. Levi props himself up and almost tips over. The sudden rush of standing up too fast.

"Now, let me double-check. Give me a sec before y'all go storming off. Hit me with a bad Google review or something."

He disappears into his upstairs room–cum-office-cum–drug den–cum–cum palace, and returns almost twenty minutes later. Watching him walk up and down the stairs is almost painful. A drunk's stumble. So many swerves and near spills. Back down, he presents a slip of wrinkled paper that has Jeremiah's mother's address scribbled on it. Mom confirms it. I take a photo with my phone because I want to document his scrawl. The slip is almost unreadable, it's so old. But it shows he returned to Lawrence after he supposedly split. Lived at this location for over a decade.

"Y'all should thank your lucky stars my documentation game is immaculate. Man of my word," Levi says, smiles. One of his canine teeth is rotten. He takes another pull from the gin gun. "You know what I'm saying, cowboy? That's me. All hat, no cattle."

I don't think that means what he thinks it means. "Sure, partner," I say.

Mom remembers the names of a few of Dad's old friends, but most don't have Internet footprints. These Gen Xers either take to the Internet in too foolhardy a way, joining everything, documenting their airport waiting periods on Snapchat, or don't have any presence at all, besides maybe a bare-bones LinkedIn profile. Each name pulls up only the slightest digital hint. A high school record of a track-and-field event with times listed. A dead link to a now-defunct rotary club. More cold trails.

Best bet now is to root around at a spot that looks like he would've frequented it. Dead end or not, we knew the risk. But since we already gassed, packed, and rode, we might as well see it through. Sometimes it's easier to hoof it to a real place in real time and cold cast for any action. Or at least that's what I learned from an Internet ghost-hunting video.

CHAPTER FIFTEEN

WE END UP at the Bottleneck, a low-standing redbrick building on New Hampshire that looks less like a live music venue and more like where you'd get a questionable tattoo. Or at least is patronized by people second-guessing their own ink. Low ceilings. Bathroom stalls with no doors. There's a show scheduled: two kids bleeping out sounds on drum pads while hidden beneath adjacent bedsheets. They look like techno ghosts.

I sidle up to the bar. Mom's freshening up in the bathroom. Nobody else is really drinking. The bedsheet show only draws six or so fans, most likely family. A bartender with downturned eyes asks me what I want to drink. She introduces herself as Virginia.

"Like the state?" she says, mockingly expecting that to be my response. The fact that the first words out of her mouth aren't about my neck either means she should be signed up for sainthood or she's working hard for that tip.

"Like the ham," is what I say. "Whiskey, no ice."

"Well?"

"Top-shelf," I say, pull out a stack of cash, but the wad is all show. It's all I have for the entire trip. Got to make three hundred last me however long this is going to take. Had to sell a bunch of DVDs to Half Price Books just to eke out enough. The stack Bojorquez had blessed me with had to pay back Mom. But pilgrimages can't have budgets, so I'm willing to dip into credit card debt if need be.

She reaches for the literal top shelf, but I stop her. Well is fine.

Virginia has a prayer-hands tattoo along her right shoulder, where the clavicle just peeks. I only spy three-quarters of it behind a dirty purple wifebeater. Over a black bra that shows its straps.

"Isn't that a man's tat?" I ask.

"What year is this?" she asks back. Seems miffed.

"I feel like I only see those hands on men in bad prison flicks."

"It's a reminder for my daily invocation," she says, assuming the position and looking up toward the heavens. "Lord, please let these cheap college kids tip well. Please let these dudebros dare not ask about my tattoos."

"I'm sorry I raised such a dummy," Mom says, sitting next to me on a bar stool, wiping her hands on tissue from her purse, the hand dryer in the bathroom clearly not doing its job. She must've caught the last bit of our convo. Or maybe this is a ready-made apology she always makes after me.

"Oh, this your boy?" Virginia asks. "Cute."

"I thought I raised him better, but you can never tell how they'll act in the wild."

"Like animals," she says, pours one for Mom. Waits a beat, pretends she isn't going to pour one for me, but then does. It's a heavy pour, too, like the bottle is made of lead.

After a few shots, I can tell she's easing on me.

"What's your favorite drink?" I ask.

"Green chartreuse," she says, point-blank.

"Three."

"It's made by monks," she says, before serving Mom and me and taking down her own. She lets out a little yip.

"As many of those as you want, on me, to get me out of the dog-house," I say.

"Who says you're there?" she asks, winks.

A man walks up and takes a seat on the empty stool next to Mom. He's handsome in a guru way. Thick but well-groomed beard, deep tan, and lots of silver neck jewelry. He seems vaguely Asian. Filipino? "Moscow," he says, matter of fact. I can tell by Mom's pause that she thinks, like me, he's ordering the fancy drink in a copper mug. He waits like he's expecting her to answer. "Lena?" she says, almost as a question.

Eventually, Mom and Moscow turn their bodies toward each other, close off the rest of us to any of their conversation. Weird to witness firsthand her flirting with this man who looks to be about twenty years younger. I pick up the convo with Virginia. She's an easy talker, which is probably part of the job description. Underneath the bullet point: takes no guff. She also has one of those raspy voices that I've heard can be a by-product of a colicky baby wailing until it has done permanent vocal cord damage. We talk past, present, and future. The kind of raw-dog honesty you can get away with in the company of a stranger.

At first, the good-time feels and full-body flush from the alcohol make me forget my circumstance: not the dad search, but my giant neck apparatus. Then I suddenly remember as I catch Virginia glance at it, but out of awkwardness or customer-service kindness, she looks away.

"I've been waitressing in this place for four years, and I keep telling myself I'm going to save up just enough to leave. I can't take it anymore. Their shitty tips. Pissy attitudes when they've had too many. Entitled assholes from small towns who move to an even whiter town for four years," Virginia says. "I need to get out."

"Where would you go?"

"Nashville. Open up my own nail salon. Play Spanish guitar as a side gig."

I want her to come with me, or I want to talk her into one night of rough-and-tumble on whatever cheap sheets she has at home. Or maybe I just want to hold her hand while she tells me about my moon sign.

"So, what's next?" she asks.

When we walk up to my car, Moscow lets out a whistle while running his finger along the body, like the paint is going to be wet. "Nice ride," he says. Our foursome get into my cramped Mustang and drive to a vague destination Virginia's being coy about. Virginia sits next to me in the passenger seat. Mom and Moscow relax in the back. I catch glimpses of them on the drive when I glance back in the rearview mirror. Laughing intimately. Heads touching. Am I on a date with my mom? I'm too enamored with Virginia to think about the weirdness of it all. She'll be the first woman I've been with since Frankie, the first woman to even give me eyes since I've had this neck attachment.

Virginia guides me first to a corner store, then the destination. She makes eye contact with them in the back, but mostly keeps her gaze laser-focused on me. Like when a little kid unwraps a new toy and can't stop staring. Now that certain boundaries have been broken, she's actually stroking the back of my head, grazing my collar with her hand.

We approach a small bungalow; it's red-and-white-trimmed and shaded by young elms. The neighborhood is quaint and lined with similar-style homes; one of them has a wagon wheel in the front yard next to a mailbox. Another has two dark-stained rocking chairs on the front porch.

We park a little ways away from the home, and Virginia waves us forward. She seems to know her way around. Or at least acts like it. Confident as a dictator. She walks past a big bush and runs her hand through it like saying hi to an old friend.

Mom and Moscow walk a few paces behind us. I'm right behind Virginia. In the dark for a split second, and I only notice it this instant, she appears like Frankie from behind. Similar height, similar shape. I feel a pang of guilt, but sleeper hold that shit. Now is not the time for soft steps and second-guesses.

When we get close to the home, Virginia reaches around this too-low fence and pops the gate.

"Who lives here?" I ask, trying to keep my voice down. It's at least two a.m. at this point, and the only noise in the quiet neighborhood is crickets and the soft scrabble of a raccoon down the street.

"Someone famous."

"What?"

"Don't worry, he's not home."

"How do you know?"

"He's dead."

We picked up package: a twelver of Bud, a bottle of Jim Beam, a bottle of cheap champagne, and a bottle of Fernet for Mom. Also a bunch of red grapes. The champagne was Virginia's call. "To celebrate," she said, but she never said what we're celebrating. Moscow grabbed the grapes. Said we needed to eat something fresh to stay alive.

"I used to walk the dog of the homeowner," Virginia whispers.

In the backyard, there's a kidney-shaped pool that looks like it hasn't been cleaned in months. Adirondack chairs and a low table are covered in leaves and dirt. Deflated water wings underneath one of the chairs. A pool skimmer lies in the tall grass. Mosquitoes hang in thick clouds.

Moscow takes out a lighter and ignites a piece of loose paper next to a fire pit. He expertly stokes the fire. "Helps with the bloodsuckers," he says, fanning the flames.

Virginia walks up to the pool's edge, dips a toe in, then gets sexy up to her ankle in the muck.

She seems satisfied, turns around, pulls off her clothes, and jumps into the pool, mismatched bra and panties on. Laundry-day underwear, but she still looks sexy as an Instagram model. I have to go after her. It takes me a sec, well, actually, way more than that—minutes—to maneuver past my cervical collar, but eventually I toss all my shit in a pile and wade in boxers-only. As I ease in, I'm fully aware of how stupid my body looks, especially with this giant weight around my neck. Also, I've avoided even looking at my naked body in so long, at least since I'd been strapped up. And I'm not looking at myself, but I know Virginia is eyeing me, so I'm so much more attuned to every stray hair, every new fold.

Virginia swims up to me and kisses me aggressively. She wraps her hands around the collar. "It's like I'm making out with an android."

She only pauses to turn to Mom and Moscow and asks if they are coming in. "The water's fine," she says, although the water is definitely not fine. It is cold as shit and feels dirty the way the edges of a bathtub with mildew feel all slimy. It feels like it's full of STDs. But a beautiful girl with prison-dude tattoos tells you to jump into a pool, you ask, *headfirst, cannonball, or belly flop?*

Also, I don't want to see Mom shimmy out of her threads. Don't get me wrong, I'm not shit-talking Mom's bod or anything. She's only forty-five and spry. Got into the yoga craze early, vinyasa-ed her way through the early nineties. When yoga pants were high-hipped, animal-patterned spandex, instead of single-tone butt advertisements. She has a core so solid, nuclear reactors run jealous.

Still, no one wants to see more of their parents physically than need be. Hell, if she went the rest of her life wearing a potato sack, I'd be fine.

I think Mom understands, and although she isn't against embarrassing me, she knows it isn't time to reveal the goods.

She grabs the bottle of Fernet, takes a seat on an Adirondack. Moscow joins her.

I should be red as hell from the public displays of affection in front of Mom, but she's engaged in her own fling, and again, I'm under that mysterious buzz of alcohol and pheromones. Virginia, on top of kissing me, grabs me underwater. She takes my dick in her hand and slowly strokes it. I give a quick whimper like a tiny cat first into the sunlight. Lucky, Mom and Moscow are downing drinks when I look over. For some reason, he has his shirt off.

"You and your mom are so cool," Virginia says.

"Do we have to talk about my mom right now?"

"I'm just saying. Both my mom and dad were assholes. I left home at fourteen."

"That bad?"

"I went through what they called a phase. Told them I was bisexual. They told me to enroll in this pray-the-gay-away camp or get the fuck out."

"Jesus."

"No, that would've kept me in. Anyway, it's cool that you can drink and hang out with your mom."

"She had me when she was young, and we've always been close."

I kiss her to try and change the subject; would prefer to ignore any Mom thoughts. Virginia grabs my hand and intersects her fingers between mine. That's when I feel it. The rock.

Should be second nature to single dudes to notice the landscape: peel an eye for a ring. I'm normally hyperaware of such signs, but I think in my current state I'm oblivious or trying to ignore the obvious. It's a weird one, too. Nothing gaudy. I almost don't recognize it for what it is because beyond the particular black braided pattern of the actual ring, the rock itself is green.

She sees me seeing it. "Peridot," she says, as if it's no big deal.

Right before I'm going to ask her the question, Moscow calls out. We both turn toward him and he's stretched out, a grape snug in his belly button. He flicks it with his finger and it soars perfectly to Virginia. She snaps at it with her head and barely misses it. It plops into the water.

"Another," she says. He loads up another. Arcs it perfectly into her mouth.

They do this one more time while Mom and I watch.

Suddenly, I'm soaked from the splash as Moscow dives into the pool. When he comes up for air, he's waist-deep, and from what I can tell he's completely naked or at least that's what I'm imagining is underneath the breach of pool water. He could be wearing swimsuit trunks that have a dick and bush laser-printed on them, but I'm guessing that's not the case. Also, I can see it move underwater. It's that big. Somewhere in a dry Kansas field, a cult all wearing the same Nikes is chanting to it.

Mom slides in after him. He's holding Mom's hand, and Mom is tipsy; I can tell because she has that flush in her cheeks and shiny-eyed look of a woman up for getting weird in a famous stranger's backyard.

Moscow dips down and lets his head go under. He streams back up on the other side of Virginia and points over at Mom. He gives her the come-here finger move. He's also got a ring on. Black metal braid. Peridot center. He puts his arm around Virginia and she says, "Ope. Hello." Conscious move or not, I slowly drift away from them and move closer to the edge of the stairs.

You ever find yourself in an awkward situation and the only thing you can think is, *What do I do with my hands?*

Moscow kisses Virginia. Deep tongue. Like uncomfortable, besides the fact that she and I were just kissing. He's also staring at me. Not sure if he's trying to gauge my reaction or he's into me. I did get a fresh haircut right before we left for the trip.

Mom's swaying and still holding Moscow's other hand. She's entranced by the twosome and probably forgot I was there. I know Mom's been truthful with me over the years, but she didn't fill me in on all the particulars regarding drug use and sexual conquests, which, I'm all for being up front, but none of us need to know bedroom facts from blood family.

The lovely couple have their paws on Mom. Moscow and Virginia with their tongues running wild. Pink as a piece of bubble gum they're swapping between them. Mom's lost in it all, and I look away. Then the two make eyes at me, wave me over. That's when Mom snaps to and is aware of what's going on; she stops in her tracks. She probably thought I would've left or that Virginia and I were gonna break off and do our own thing. It's odd all the way around, but who am I to deny her?

Only once it dawns on both of us that they don't want to keep things separate, they want us all on the same merry-go-round, Mom and I make eye contact and acknowledge that it's time to go. As in, let's smash a bottle of alcohol on the ground and fucking run.

Mom flings off all limbs, and briskly gets out. I'm halfway up the swimming pool steps, trying to find my shoes in the dark.

"Way past my bedtime," Mom says, a parting shot on a cordial note.

"Relax a little," Moscow says.

I always figured if it got far enough with a married woman, she'd better tell me. And now she's telling me. She and Moscow are married.

"We want all of us to enjoy each other's company," Virginia and Moscow say almost in unison, which only adds to the creep factor. Likely a line they pull out all the time, but the chorus is for the wrong crowd.

"Nope," Mom says. "Ricky?"

Mom and I awkwardly gather our things: clothes, keys, wallets. The two of them watch us and bob in the water. I can't properly bend, so I snatch up what I can, but Mom is shouldering the load, holding almost all our things. I loosely grip a shirt that waves behind me like a flag.

"Get in," Moscow says. "Let's relax and forget this little setback."

"A setback is a flat tire. This is a goddamned train wreck," I say, already heading for the gate.

Mom and I walk barefoot through the streets holding our shoes. We want to get out of there as quickly as possible. Leave it all behind and never speak of it again. Although I thought we were on the same wavelength with the whole let's-never-discuss-this, Mom starts talking as soon as we're inside the car. The dome light shines on us looking like a pair of wet dogs with our matted hair. Mom has a stray leaf poking out of her head.

"Well, that was—"

"Weird."

"Silly."

"What?" I ask.

"A few drinks. Met some new people."

"New people? Some sicko and his wife trying to bamboozle us into mom-on-son action." I shut the door so we're back in the dark. Start the engine.

"It would've never gotten that far," Mom says, wrings water out of her hair and flicks it out the window. Tosses the leaf.

"Did you not see what I saw? You were there. I was there. We were all there."

"Oh, Ricky. You have to live a little."

"Incest isn't on my bucket list. Nowhere near my bucket," I say. Slowly drive down side streets while my phone loads a map.

"Of course not. But sometimes it's about seeing how the night unfolds. They thought they were steering, but we had all the power to pump the brakes. C'mon, Ricky, you think your mom rolls over for anyone?"

"Next time we need to have a code," I say, praying there's never a next time. "Geronimo. Anything. Those motherfuckers tried to *Criss Angel Mindfreak* us." I turn onto a street that leads to another street that leads to another state.

"It's a story, if anything," Mom says, laughs.

With our newest small-town lead and feeling the leftover ick of an attempted incest orgy, I hightail it out of Lawrence. Leave the Rock Chalk and head west. Mom says she remembers where Jeremiah lived in Colorado.

"You still remember?" I ask.

"I'll recognize it when we get close," she says.

While we still have the sluggishness of booze in our systems and probably shouldn't be driving, the circumstances are a jolt to the system. Affords us a few hours to coast early into Colorado, when the roads are mostly empty minus a few lone headlights hitting us with intermittent shine and the intruding rumble of semis as they zoom by.

CHAPTER SIXTEEN

WE DIP INTO the midsection of Kansas as thunderstorms light up the empty plains, when Mom feels the need to get confessional. I'm listening but also keeping an eye out as lightning cracks every few minutes and flashes on rolling hills and the occasional copse of trees. I can't imagine what it would be like to be out in Tornado Alley with little to no coverage and a twister bearing down on you or even making a cameo nearby. It happens all the time in Kansas and Missouri. Makes tinder and kindling out of whole townships. While we aren't strangers to tornado weather in Omaha, it's far too hilly and building-saturated for any real wind to build up a head of steam. One time in high school there was a tornado warning when I was working at Westroads Mall and they had to have all the patrons and workers safely ushered onto the lowest level, which at the time was a giant arcade, so I played *NBA Jam* for an hour while we waited for the threat to pass. In Omaha, at most a tornado jiggles a shingle or bullies a small tree out of the ground, but even that's rare. In open

Kansas pasture, it feels like you have a bull's-eye on your back and Mother Nature's just waiting to take aim.

We drive quickly while hail belts the car and pings little divots into the clear coat.

"Ricky, I'm sorry that was a dead end. I was pretty sure there was going to be some juice there. I wasn't being completely honest with you that I never touched base with Jeremiah. Well, checked in on. There were times over the years, especially recently when the Internet made it so much easier, that I would type his name into a search engine or Facebook. Not a lot. A few times over the years. Especially nights when I had hard questions or even too much to drink and felt that ninth beer work its tricks on my judgment. I didn't contact him or anything. Just glanced at a picture or two. Checked in on where he worked. He likes the movies *Young Guns* and *Deerhunter*. Also, he was working at a textile plant in Colorado Springs, and a newspaper interviewed him and his fellow machinists because apparently they all bought into this lottery and hit big on the state for three point five million divided by thirty people. He was usually in on the pool but didn't go that day. I think it only ended up being like one hundred twenty thousand dollars per person but no one was willing to give him a shake."

I want to tell Mom, *Trust me, I know what it's like to creep on a past love through social media.* But I don't say anything. Let the rain patter against the windshield make the sound effects. I'm frustrated coming up empty-handed. Upset that we wasted our time. Still a little aroused thinking about Virginia. But also disgusted that I'm the least bit blood-flushed after all that.

A bolt shows us what I-70 West designs look like in the daytime. Trees that look like arterial maps of hands.

"So, did you know he wasn't in Lawrence?"

"No, like I said, there's only a little information available. I thought he could've been in Lawrence. Or at least someone in Lawrence might've known his whereabouts. That or Lamar. He used to have family in Lamar. It's a little Podunk town of a few hundred, maybe a few thousand people at most. I'm talking less than five stoplights. A diner. A little downtown."

"Have you been there before?"

"One time, when Jeremiah and I were dating, we did a bunch of blow . . . got all hopped up . . . he told me he loved me and that he wanted me to meet his mom . . . at like one a.m. we decided to leave right then and there and drive through the night. Like we're doing now, I guess. We blasted a few rails for the road . . . took off in his little Volvo . . . pulled into town at like eight a.m. We drove straight to his mother's place, which was a beautiful ranch house on fifteen acres of land . . . barely any neighbors . . . they were so far from each other. You had to drive up this winding hill that was barely a road, and little jackrabbits skittered past us every twenty feet . . . tumbleweeds the size of small couches. His mom had lucked out because she'd been an elementary school teacher her entire life with bold ambitions of retiring to Colorado. But on her schoolteacher's salary, there's no way she could've afforded a place out there . . . What had happened was that she had once passed through Lamar at the age of twelve and had deemed it so beautiful that she had saved her entire life just to get back. And she lucked out . . . A gentleman and his wife had grandiose plans of beginning their lives there, but apparently the wife was pretty big . . . Doctors would peg her as obese. And the husband thought that fresh mountain air would do her good . . . She couldn't even go from one floor to the next without wheezing horribly. She forced him to sell, and Jeremiah's mom picked it up for pennies at the right time. So Jeremiah and I show up at his mom's door at eight a.m. . . . . bleary-eyed . . . reeking of cigarettes because we chain-smoked the entire time . . . shaky from the comedown."

Mom tells me over the course of two hours. Stopping and starting. Stopping sometimes even for minutes at a stretch and drumming her fingers on the dash, collecting her thoughts. I stay quiet the entire time, afraid that if I chime in, it might break the chain.

She says that the worst part was that in the cold light of the morning, the whole idea had burned out from a good idea to a bad time. She didn't really know Jeremiah's mom. His mom didn't know Lena. Jeremiah and Lena weren't serious enough for a meet-the-parents seven-hour road trip. The last two hours they both knew it was bad news, but were afraid to say anything. Didn't utter a word all through the eastern edge of Colorado. Smoked in silence. By the time they arrived at his mom's house, the thrill was gone and they were both wanting to return to Lawrence. The beginning of the end. His mom was nice enough. They stayed for a night before driving back. She made them waffles in the morning.

"It was a real pretty town, though. Real pretty," Mom says. Tapers off. The last thing she's going to say on the subject.

Mom drifts off after that, and I turn on the radio to listen to Delilah and hear about a stranger's Christian ails. I white-knuckle it through every boom of thunder, grip it and rip it, hoping every crack of lightning is the last. I pray for sunup and the fade into that early morning blue-white sky like in a vanilla-flavored coffee creamer ad.

At some point in the night-to-morning blur, we switch positions. Mom in her motherly know-it-allness simply intones, "Switch," and we make the switch. She can tell I'm on my last bar. At some points, I may have been driving with my eyes closed. I don't even fuss; I pull over at the nearest shoulder and we change places. Rest my head against the cool passenger-side window. Soon as I'm buckled in, I nod off. Saw that log heavy.

When I wake, Mom's squatting by the side of the highway, peeing free. Or at least that's what it sounds like from her hiding in bushes set back from the road. Her pants are around her ankles, I assume, because she almost falls over and yells out, "Goddammit."

"Where are we?" I ask, my breath like it killed someone and buried the body inside my mouth. The film on my teeth feels like each tooth is sporting its own wool coat.

"The timing's bad," Mom says. "We'd get into town too early. And I want to take a little detour to see the smartest woman in Kansas."

CHAPTER SEVENTEEN

HALSTEAD, KANSAS, IS a blip on the map. A wooden sign announces it as THE BIGGEST LITTLE CITY IN KANSAS. As we roll into town, my phone notes that the population is basically a big high school. Under two thousand. My graduating class was six hundred kids. We could've crushed this city.

Best I can make out, it's a couple of grain elevators, a water tower, a steepled church, some small neighborhoods, a railroad track that cuts right through.

We pull up to a drab rectangle of a building that reads KANSAS LEARNING CENTER FOR HEALTH. I grip a Styrofoam cup of gas station coffee we grabbed on the way in. Have to wear my sunglasses indoors, because I don't want anyone to see my bloodshot eyes.

"Mom, hate to break it to you, but it's a little late for the talk."

"Not why we're here. Also, remember I was the first person to give you condoms."

"Who else would've?"

We walk inside, and it's clearly been remodeled in the past few years. Makes me glad for my glasses. While the outside is a gray rectangle, the inside is all brightly colored walls and exhibits. Checkerboard floors, lime-green-and-purple motifs. Giant-size, child-friendly displays showing the inner workings of the nose, eyes, mouth. Everything is Skittles bright.

"I haven't been here in years," Mom says. She looks as new to it all as me. "There's my girl," she says, and walks to a far corner. Follows a sign into a small auditorium.

I almost drop my coffee. Her "girl" is a see-through mannequin of a young woman with her skeleton and other insides visible to the world. She's positioned on a spinning pedestal and presenting her different organs; as each organ is discussed, it lights up. Her name is Valeda: The Transparent Talking Woman. A sign informs us that in a naming contest, she'd almost been christened Lucid Lil or Cassie the Lassie with the Glassy Chassis. I know winning names, and that last one is an ace. Probably would've upped their revenue by fifteen percent.

What a gimmick. If only a wrestler wrestled in a skintight suit that showed his or her organs like that Jew-fro'd weirdo Slim Goodbody, who I used to watch as a child on public access television. That shit was frightening and educational.

We take front-row seats to watch the exhibit. I point to my neck. "Are you sure she's not my mom?"

"I used to come out here whenever I lived in Lawrence and headed anywhere out west. I think she's beautiful.

"Also, you have to remember, pre-Internet, it was hard to really learn about your body as a young woman. My mom took me here when I was a kid and planted me in front of this thing. Instead of just telling me. That's why I was always straightforward with you. Don't do this. Don't be afraid of that. Stop touching that thing." Mom whispers like we're in church.

Mom recites parts of the robot's speech with her. Apparently, it hasn't changed.

I suck on the dregs of my coffee, feel the grit between my teeth.

Mom rests her head on my shoulder. Even that little shift sends a shock of pain through my body. But I can't shake off Mom. I let her rest. In a few minutes, she's lightly snoring. Valeda moves on to the pancreas.

I let Mom sleep through the rest of the spiel, and when Valeda is done, I gently rouse her. We drift through the center: breeze through Charlie Bones, a skeleton exhibit, and eye a real iron lung; right before we hit the road, Mom grabs my phone. "Better camera," she says. She walks up to the men's restroom and props the door open with her foot. "Anyone in here?" she asks. "Piss and get out." She barks this in a faux-dude voice. No one replies. It's early and we are the only ones in the entire place, minus a few chipper-looking staff.

She ducks into the restroom, lets the door flap behind her, and in two minutes she's back out, whistling. I stay directly outside as eagle eye, as lookout.

She tosses my phone at me.

"Hey, watch it," I say, as I snatch the phone, one-handed, in the air. Even that quick action hurts. I barely move my body besides my arm, but this situation I have going on stifles every movement. Lucky I didn't drop it.

I scroll through my photos and see three quick snaps of what appears to be granite or stone that's badly etched into. The first one is blurry. The photos read JT, a heart shape, LP. Jeremiah Twohatchet loves Lena Powell. Probably etched with a penknife.

"Why didn't you just send me in?" I ask.

"It's in a secret spot. A little corner that we hoped would give it the best chance of lasting. Also, you wouldn't have been able to get the angle with that turtleneck."

"Did y'all stop here before that trip out to his mom's?" I wonder aloud.

Mom doesn't reply, whistles as she walks. Smooth as a cowboy in an ad for cast-iron pans.

We get back in the Mustang, crank country radio to keep us awake, and get on the interstate to Lamar. Mom drives while I fiddle with the stations. Some guy twangs about heartbreaks and alibis. We pass billboards for antique shop pull-offs, strip club coaxes, and JESUS SAVES signs. Someone's full Sunday platter.

CHAPTER EIGHTEEN

NEBRASKA IS PRETTY flat, although not as flat as Kansas. About Kansas, I once heard someone say that you could watch your dog run away from you for three days straight.

The highways and interstates through the middle of the country ease my mind. It's not a scenic drive, point out the postcard beauty. But it's definitely a zen, clear-headed kind of scroll. Drives out east are too bumper-to-bumper near big cities. Also, there are way too many tolls. I once paid seventeen dollars and fifty cents in Ohio because I pulled over at a rest stop to get a slice of cold pizza. The drive down south is more picturesque, but it doesn't let you exist in your own head. You're always peering at a river town in Arkansas or leering at weirdos in Louisiana. Go past the panhandle in Nebraska and you're automatically in the mountains. Purple in their majesty.

But that boring block in the Midwest that most doze through is my favorite part. I'm probably biased, because I've spent so many years zigzagging through them. Come across a horizon of waving grain and

I want to pull over and run toward it until I can't see any more road. Where there's nothing but green-and-yellow patchwork grass and the rest of the world seems swallowed up.

Whenever I'd pass through Boston or Connecticut for a wrestling bid, they'd be amazed that road trips that we took were regularly twelve to fifteen hours or more. The east is so scrunched, I was once in Massachusetts when they blared a tornado warning for a twister in Connecticut.

Also the skies in the Midwest beat all. They're so wide open. My grandpa grew up near the ocean in Oregon. Although I never knew him that well, he taught me how to skip rocks and tie a jig. After he and Grandma split, he's been living in Oklahoma for forty years. Whenever he sees a big body of water, he goes back to being a boy. I get it. I feel no pangs, because I'm Nebraska born, Nebraska raised. Landlocked. No coast. But the sky calls to me. When I'm in a big city, especially out east, I hate how the sky is always encumbered by a dumb-ass building budging into my periphery. Get the fuck out of here, you goddamned rectangle.

Also, because Nebraska is next to Iowa, land of the wind turbine, it's not rare to see the flashing lights of a WIDE LOAD caravan rushing past you on the highway, followed by a blade or two from a turbine. Even though they're man-made, there's something awesome about being close to something that big; I imagine that's what it's like to come across a beached whale carcass and roll by its bones.

I once worked for four weeks on a quick run crew maintaining those turbines on a wind farm, and I still get gooseflesh seeing them disassembled and roaring down the highway. The whole trip was a trip. You get fully geared up. Hard hat. Hooks and straps. Pass a climbing test. I had to learn how to climb without tiring out my arms. Don't pull yourself up so much as you pull yourself toward the ladder. Nothing like seeing the world from that perch: all those slow blades spinning like there's nothing more important than the next breeze.

It's easy to take all that flat land for granted. Until you see it from the eyes of someone full of wonder. I remember when the Intertribal Council kids were planning a bake sale to raise money to visit an out-of-state powwow. They also wanted to hit the Mid-America All-Indian Center in Wichita. It's a five-hour drive that cuts straight down through Kansas, none too beautiful as far as American vistas go. But when they returned, they couldn't stop talking about how incredible it was.

"Holy shit, Ricky!" Pilgrim said. "All that space." He spread his arms wide. Most of them had rarely had the opportunity to travel. Some had never set foot on an airplane. A few never went beyond the borders of Nebraska or Iowa. Even Kansas was alien to them, and although I'd covered those roads so many times, I sat back and listened to how they were dazzled by the same pastures. I couldn't help but see them fresh. Like when a wide-eyed child gets excited and describes blue to you in a new way.

CHAPTER NINETEEN

ROADS AND SKY aside, growing up in Nebraska and Iowa, being born in Des Moines and then moving to Lincoln and eventually Omaha, I've mostly been surrounded by white people. Des Moines and Lincoln have heavy Vietnamese and Southeast Asian populations, but I don't mingle with them much besides one summer when I was asked to join a Laotian basketball rec team because I knew a dude and they were thin on the bench.

While I look white as a Republican, I've always prided myself on being half-Native. Having some Native blood makes me feel special, like I stand out from the crowd. Gives me a sense of self.

It didn't help that Mom tended to mythologize Jeremiah. I'd do pretty generic things like crack my knuckles individually with each hand and then join them together and bow them palms-out and she'd look all dreamy-eyed and say, "That's just like how your dad used to do it." She did it less and less as I got older, but when I was growing up and still taking shape as a human, she'd point out our similarities in both personality and physical frame. How we swept our hair. How we held our arms over our heads when hard of breath. Meanwhile, huge chunks of the general population do those same things. Literally anyone who ever got that arm advice from their middle school gym teacher after running the mile.

I began feeling a sense of pride in my Native side come high school. By that time wrestling had been a hobby that a buddy of mine, Yuri, and I had been into big. Yuri and I had similar stories. We grew up, separately, watching eighties names turn into nineties has-beens, cobbling together rings for our action figures with Popsicle sticks, tape, and twine. Then faded out of it for a few years in middle school, when rap and rock and budding girls' bodies interested us more. High school saw a renewed interest, not just by us, but also by the public. Wrestling had bypassed the eighties headliners we'd watched on home videos and was moving into another generation of loudmouths and personas that summed up the nineties perfectly: the Attitude Era. Stone Cold, The Rock, D-Generation X. WWE was hot again. Wrestling dominated TV. The Monday Night Wars.

Yuri and I made a plywood ring frame that rested on air mattresses in my backyard. We were doing what we did as kids but on a bigger scale. Mom was fine with it. She was busy trying to resurrect her dating life and said that as long as we weren't shooting heroin, we were fine. TV told her that heroin was available at every corner store. We just wanted to do leaps from the top rope. We smoked weed on occasion, but at that age, we mostly wanted to catch air and jerk off. Although not in combo.

We watched classic matches on VHS: Hogan vs. Andre the Giant, Bret Hart vs. Shawn Michaels, Shawn Michaels vs. Razor Ramon. Rented Wrestlemanias with popcorn and Red Vines from Blockbuster. We wore them down so much through replaying and rewinding that they showed signs of wear and tear. Fuzzy lines and tracking issues.

We choreographed our own fights. Spent hours drinking Gatorade and working out our issues in the ring.

Sophomore year, the school hosted a talent show. Yuri and I signed up as The Go Big Reds. Yuri dressed up as his alter ego, Bolo, and I dressed up as mine, Old Chief Smoke. Old Chief Smoke was the name of an actual Great Sioux chief, but I only picked it because I thought I was being slick with the weed reference. I was head to toe in knockoff Native garb coupled with sunglasses, socks, and a necklace that were all emblazoned with marijuana leaves. I bought bad Indian costumes at costume shops and made a slapdash one out of three. I painted my face and wore moccasins. I didn't catch flack over the weed nods in my costume until later, because I waited to don the clothes and accessories until right before we strode onstage. Bolo was Yuri's take on eighties Commie stereotypes. He knew the slurs hurled, because, well, his name was Yuri, and he wanted to give it back to them a little bit. Calling our crew The Go Big Reds was a not-so-subtle jab at the Huskers, and also, we figured, there was an additional layer to us upending stereotypes about both our folks. It took a long time for us to hash that out, and also, Yuri was on a big metaphor kick because Miss Grisham, his English teacher, once said he "showed promise" in his poems.

Yuri and I did a five-minute choreographed routine while "We Are the Champions" played in the background. The crowd ate it up. They were hooting and hollering. Most of the other stuff kids did was bad skits or neck Hula-Hooping or sad garage-band anthems. One girl did a cover of Natalie Imbruglia's "Torn." I won the match and ran around high-fiving my peers. Come to think of it, years later, I'm not sure if they were laughing with us or at us. Still, in that moment, I knew the glory of adulation. I never wanted to come off that mountain. Unfortunately, we didn't win. We were disqualified due to my "questionable" apparel choices. The girl who did "Torn" got first. She received a medal and a pass to skip study hall, but I envied the roar. Found out years later that

"Torn" is a cover, meaning she did a cover of a cover, which, twenty-twenty, cheapens the deal. We should've won.

Yuri and I drifted down different paths: I kept up wrestling and he got into cars. Full-on gearhead. We're Facebook friends in that way where once a year, when I log on to double-check the start time of an event, I'll see Yuri post a photo of himself crouched and giving a thumbs-up next to his souped-up Mazda. Maybe I click like. Maybe I don't. I think he's a Realtor by day. No bad blood. That dude was in my corner when I first felt that dopamine kick from a crowd cheering my name. I'll never forget that. Also, fuck "Torn." The original, I mean. The Natalie Imbruglia one is untouchable.

CHAPTER TWENTY

MOM AND I roll into Lamar at a respectable hour, midafternoon, the sun still high and heavy. Even with the AC on, at this altitude, it feels like we are close enough to grab it out of the air. Pocket it for a rainy day.

We wind through town and Mom points out little coffee shops, antique places with hand-painted signs. It doesn't seem like it's changed since she'd been here last. She remembers it down to the details like a fridge-hung postcard. She'd only been here once, but the town imprinted itself on her.

We stop at an intersection, where an elderly couple take their sweet time crossing. The old man in an oversize cardigan drops a half-peeled grapefruit he's palming and slowly gets after it. Normally, I'd be pissed, but in this town, the genteel nature is part of the scenery. I feel like I'm watching a cartoon turtle. Mom gives them a wave.

We drive up to a fenced-off area on the outskirts. Past a bush and then another bush. Mom buzzes a number. Wrong one. She tries again. An old lady's voice comes across the intercom: "Who is it?"

"This is about Jeremiah," Mom says.

We get buzzed in.

We drive another mile and a half up and down winding paths. The path isn't a real road as much as it is gravel scattered in swaths meant to give a semblance of direction. Pebbles ping off the wheel wells and fenders. Little lizards and rabbits dash in front of us. We try to miss as many as possible, but we definitely hear the crunch of something underneath, even barely rolling at an easygoing fifteen miles an hour, if that.

At first we take a wrong turn. Went left when we should've steered right. Or maybe Mom does it on purpose, because she stops in a driveway of a home that clearly isn't our destination, then parks the car and turns to me. "You sure you're ready for this?"

"No turning back now."

"Okay, just want to make sure you're good." Then we double back onto the right road.

We pull into the driveway of an old ranch home. Southwestern adobe–style with plants outside dying in the heat. The grass hasn't been mowed in some time, but also most of it has dried in small brown patches like God himself played bully with a magnifying glass. An overturned, empty flowerpot sits on the lawn alongside a rusted rake and a half-deflated basketball. One of those old sprinklers that arcs the water in a high back-and-forth rainbow pattern looks like it hasn't been turned on since ever. Overgrown with grass and fossilized into the landscape.

An older woman appears fuzzy behind glass. She opens the door slowly and steps out.

She has long black hair with gray streaks in it. Her eyes are sunken into her face in that way that old age will retreat you. I expected her, probably due to my own projected bullshit, to be dressed more ornately, but other than a colorful beaded necklace and earrings, she's wearing typical grandma garb: an old thrifted T-shirt that reads LAKE TAHOE, USA, and a blue chambray shirt over it with the sleeves rolled up.

She stands there, silent, while Mom and I approach. No one says anything for a few seconds. Though those seconds seem to last forever. I feel like I could've taken a shit in between the pause. Not just like a quick one, either: solid reading, summarized a few articles after.

"Come inside," she says finally.

We step inside and it smells like sandalwood. But not the honest essence, more a candle that was lab fabricated. Animal skulls line most flat surfaces. Even post on walls. An empty turtle shell is shellacked and propped against a wall like a suit of clothes a naked-ass turtle left behind in a hurry. A lot of tiny things carved out of heavy woods. Doilies, now that I know what they are, are underneath or on top of everything.

She motions for us to sit down at a large oak table that's off-colored and covered in scratches.

"Coffee? Tea?"

"Coffee's fine," both Mom and I say. The woman makes a cup of her own tea. Looks like twigs and dirt. She hands us two mugs of the standard stuff. We're both sitting down, but she elects to stand. Swirls a small spoon in her mug.

"So, Jeremiah," the woman says. "What are y'all offering?"

"Uhm, what do you want from us?" Mom asks, clearly confused.

"Oh, is this the game?"

"I'm sorry, what are you asking?" I ask.

"Oh, the youngblood chimes in. Good cop, bad cop. Trying to push around an old woman."

"Push around an old woman?" I ask.

"You think this is my first rodeo, junior?"

"Maggie," says Mom.

"So, you know my name. Sure you got that in a file somewhere. Don't think that move will bring me to kowtow to something lowball."

"Maggie, it's Lena."

"Listen, I grew up on a farm. You know you never name the slaughter. I named them all. I also ate them. No wool over this woman's eyes. Try another one." She seems almost angry. Her voice gets louder, and her mug gives a slight shake.

"Lena, it's Lena. Arlene Powell. I dated Jeremiah for a short stint over twenty years ago."

The woman starts talking over Mom. Doesn't hear a word she says. "This is what they do. They take and they take and they take. Never gave him a real chance. An honest chance. And now that they know they might have to pony up, they're trying to back an old woman into a corner. They"—and she looks directly at us now—"you. You take and take. He just wanted a fighting chance." She physically slumps, her shoulders hunch, and she looks like she's about to coil back or crumple straight to the ground.

"What? What happened to Jeremiah?" I ask.

She's slouched over for a good minute. Then slowly straightens back up. We give her this silence. "Did you say Lena? From way back when?"

"Yes, Maggie. It's Lena," Mom says.

It dawns on her. It dawns all over her. She seems to relax for a second. But then a new look crosses her face. Like she got a whiff of something that reeks but isn't trying to show it.

"What are you doing here? And who's the kid?"

"We were looking for Jeremiah. Have you heard from Jeremiah?" Mom asks.

The woman looks me up and down.

"He's his boy," Mom says.

"This boy looks white as a snowman."

"Well, he'd be old enough. Dates don't lie."

"The nose is all wrong. And the eyes. No. What about those other men you were spreading it for?"

"That's none of your business. Jeremiah wasn't exactly keeping to himself in those days, either," Mom says, a hitch in her voice. "We were young. Stupid."

"Don't talk about my boy like that," Maggie says, sets her tea down. "So why come looking for Jeremiah now? Didn't you two only date for a year?"

"My son—"

"I'm looking for him," I say, try to cut the tension.

"What happened to you, boy?" She looks me up and down. Twice. Eyes linger over my neck. "Can't stop biting?" She barely pauses. Has little filter, which means maybe we are related.

"Hurt my neck. Almost broke it."

"Is he here or not, Maggie?" Mom stops with the niceties.

"He's not here."

"Okay," Mom says, slowly stands. The drag of the bottom of her chair against the floor is too dramatic for the moment. Or maybe just dramatic enough.

"He's not anywhere."

"What?" She stops.

"He's dead, Lena. Died about a year and a half ago."

"Wow, I'm, I'm sorry, Maggie." Mom is just standing in front of her chair now.

"Had a heart attack on the job. He was working maintenance. Things were on the up. But his body couldn't maintain after years of pouring that junk through his system."

"Drink?" I ask, losing sight of my manners. "I'm so sorry, ma'am," I say, starting to stand, follow Mom's lead.

"Coca-Cola. He loved Coca-Cola. He drank seven or eight a day, every day. His coworkers celebrated him by pouring Coca-Cola out on the ground."

Not a member of the Pepsi Generation, I almost say. It's that knee-jerk reaction to undercut something solid with a joke.

Tears well in her eyes. Her arms go to her sides, and her fists clench and unclench. "They loved him at that job. They told me they'd do right by him. People were supposed to show, are going to show, who are going to cut a check. I don't care about the money. No amount will sit right. I just want enough to cover his funeral. I thought y'all were the question askers sent by corporate. But I have a feeling they're getting cold feet."

She turns away, sounds like she gives a little gasp. Accidentally tips over her mug. Instinctively, I grab out for her, want to pat her on the back, rub her shoulder, do something. She jerks away.

"You are not my blood," she says, her back to me.

CHAPTER TWENTY-ONE

MOM AND I retreat in silence back toward town. The old man is still chasing the grapefruit. No, of course he's not, but in my mind he'll forever be toddling after it. The few minutes it takes to drive into town draw out like watching water boil. A praying mantis as big as my hand catches a ride on the hood; it's locked in with its pincers, but we're so slow-going it hops off after a few miles, probably to find a quicker lift. I roll down the window, sneeze when the sun hits me directly.

"Wouldn't Facebook say he'd died?"

"That's not how it works, Mom." Damn, I'm so stunned. Maybe in my heart I want to believe Maggie is wrong or trying to mask her own pain. But I know she's right. How could I have been so stupid? We don't even look alike. I couldn't see it until she looked me dead in the eyes and told me no. *Not even close, son.*

Neither Mom nor I say anything. Unsure of what to do, we keep driving. Keep driving.

As we slow at an intersection, we both perk at lights, machinery, and loud music coming from a field. The lights throw me off because it's not yet night. It's late afternoon, and the sun is still a presence. Mom drives into the parking lot across the field as if we've done this a thousand times before.

It's a carnival set up on the outskirts of town. For whatever reason we float toward the spectacle. Dumb as moths to light. We don't discuss driving directly back. It's unspoken, but clearly we need to take a second, figure this space station will give us the right amount of pause to get things squared up for whatever's next.

Children walk around with pink cotton-candy spools, their parents poultry-fisting roasted turkey legs. People are gleeful, food juice dripping from their faces. Everything is loud: buzzy noises or kids' sugar-wild shrieks.

Rides look sketchy and rust-spotted, but children still line up to ride them and they creak and groan as they lift and whirl. I've always had carnie apprehensions, simply because the go-up and teardown are done with such speed, and also a young girl in Omaha got scalped by a malfunctioning ride, so I've felt the need to keep a respectable distance.

A makeshift rodeo is set up with hay bales cutting off the ring and clowns scattered throughout to keep a sense of order. I quickly realize that the participants are mostly inmates, probably hauled from the nearby federal pen. The supermax where the world's worst criminals who ever rubbed America wrong are pent-up. The Unabomber, crime bosses, gang leaders. They also have an adjoining, less hard-core camp that's minimum security. The guys now suited and booted walking into a possible goring or bucking for our drunken approval. Most of them haven't shaved and have tats on necks, hands, scalps.

Mom and I sit in the bleachers. The crowd around us hoots and hollers. Honest to God, someone gives a "Yee-haw!"

"Listen, Ricky, I know that was brutal. But I have to come clean . . ."

I sit on the other end of that half sentence with the biggest fucking dunce cap on.

". . . there's a chance Jeremiah wasn't your father."

"What?" I ask, not in surprise, but because I generally can't hear her. It sounds like she says something about Chance the Rapper.

"Jeremiah wasn't your father," she yells louder, at this one moment the noise dips. Those words will clang around in my head forever like the chorus of a song you listened to while losing your virginity.

"What the fuck are you talking about, Mom?"

"There's a chance it was someone else."

"Are you trying to make me feel better?"

"No, no, I never told you this because I never wanted to believe it. It was nothing against Temple, but he wasn't really my type. He was someone I was seeing between Jeremiah. We hooked up a couple of times, but it was a night here, a night there. It flamed out.

"Back in college he was really into yoga and holistic medicine; he was actually the first guy to get me into yoga, now that I think about it. He wasn't a professional or anything, he just did it in his spare time. We practiced in his studio apartment. With incense burning and the room all hot. At the time, all the stretching and breathing kicked off our relationship, but there wasn't much beyond that. Also remember that in the nineties, nobody knew what yoga was. It was foreign and cool and he would say things like 'namaste' and bang a gong over me and wave burning incense around me to cleanse my energy; he also stretched shirtless."

"All right, Mom. Too much. Too fucking much."

"I'm sorry. I'm rambling. I'm just saying, I know you're searching for something. For someone. And he might be the someone. I never meant to purposefully hide it from you; I genuinely never thought that you could be Temple's kid. And I know that means jack shit right now. I did . . . I did go along with the whole Jeremiah thing."

"Thing?"

"I know. I have to own up to that. But I wasn't trying to pull one over on you. Temple and I were nothing. What we had was a bump. I barely remember him."

"Pretty sure I was the bump," I say, rub my closed eyes with my thumbs. "I'm not sure what's worse, that you're telling me my dad is someone else or that he was a yoga instructor named Temple."

"We called him Temple, but his name is Roy. Roy Templeton. And it's yogi."

"What?"

"The term is 'yogi.'"

"Why would you never mention it until right this moment?"

"When you were a child you were dead set on your dad being some bigger-than-life superhero. Wrestler. Astronaut."

"But that's the same shit every kid wishes, Mom. You didn't think there was a time when you should've revealed the truth to me before we were literally at the doorstep of someone I thought could've been my grandma?"

"It became such a part of you. I never dreamed we'd need to find him. And I was sure it was Jeremiah, too. Either Jeremiah or Temple, and I never really considered Temple."

"What does that have to do with me?" The crowd cheers the felons bulldogging. Two men wrestle the steer to the ground in record time.

"Maybe I didn't want to consider it was anyone but Jeremiah."

"And you thought right now was the time to hit me with this?" I shift in my seat, my ass cold from the metal bleachers. Mom tries to put her hand on mine, but I reflexively pull back.

"I don't know. You seemed so destroyed back there."

"What does this guy look like?"

"I don't have any photos to show you."

"Mom, I've been thinking my dad was Native, that I was Native, pretty much my entire life. And if it turns out I'm the son of a guy named Roy, what does that mean? Fucking Roy?"

"I know, and I never needed help, so I never figured to seek either one out. You never mentioned wanting to find your father before. Also, we couldn't just Google someone until a few years ago."

"A few years ago?"

"You know what I mean. Once you bury something it's easier to let it lie than dig it up. Times are different now. Yeah, the stigma of being a single mother isn't what it once was, but even back then you'd catch looks from people who would find out. Maybe they didn't mean it, but their faces never lied. It was me and you, and that's all we needed. Until you needed a little more, I guess."

I stand up to get some space, all this information too heavy on my shoulders. I have to sit with this for a second. Hell, a minute, a month, forever.

I feel gutted. Need a bit of me time so as not to show these Colorado folks my emotions boiling over. I sneak underneath the bleachers like a high school goon. Pull out an edible that I bought from a dispensary on the drive. It was called You're Ganja Have a Good Time. Mom and I both copped edibles. I bought a chocolate-and-fig bar that was 100 mg. I also bought some salted caramels. I crack off two of the ten chocolate pieces. Fuck it, I go for three.

Mom texts me that she's going to wander, get something sweet to nosh on. She doesn't realize I'm right by her. Well, beneath the bleachers. Find her when I'm ready, she texts.

After downing the hatch, I compose my shit, go for a stroll. I'm waiting for the kick as I take in the environs. People shooting jumpers at the overly high backboards. Young men and women dressed mostly in denim holding hands or even worse, hugged up with their hands in each other's back pockets. (Open-air butt touching.) Kids trying to find their equilibrium on those horizontal rope balance ladders.

Thing about weed that Colorado has right is let people be. We're all adults here. Nebraska is meth head central. Or pills you can score from Stevie Ray, who always sits by the jukebox in the biker bar. But some people get uptight; I get it. Generations of moms and pops were weaned on those bad propaganda films. You ever see that black-and-white one where the cowpoke takes a toke and blasts holes into people? But tell me, in what world does it make sense to pop a pill or get a shot to ease pain but get fined for smoking? Neck injury aside, I know my body is built to spill. It's what I signed up for. Thank the Lord indie wrestling promos don't test for weed, but at the highest level, every athlete is scrutinized. Don't kneel during the anthem, don't speak freely on social media, don't ever take a toke. Not in God's America.

It's too early yet for the effects, so I still move my feet. Night sets in, and the too bright lights come on even stronger postdusk. We've been here for a few hours and it's been at least thirty minutes since I gnawed the chocolate. (Don't know why I bought one with figs. What the fuck is a fig?) The Ferris wheel is missing lights. The giant bounce castle seems weakly tethered to the ground. The huge stuffed animal prizes are knockoffs: Mickey Mouse's Middle Eastern cousin. Suddenly, I want to take a seat. See something familiar.

At the outer edges of the whole spectacle is a shoddy ring that a few middle-aged men are wrestling in. (Not sure if they're also criminals or drunk passersby prodded by so-called friends to sign up for a five-minute grab and spin.) They're mostly dad bods (which answers my question: the prisoners would be more yoked or at least on average more tatted, more muscular, more survival-mode streamlined) stuffed into undersized unitards worn over their own clothes. (The unis have clearly been borrowed from a local college and a costume store, because they are either over-the-top gaudy or plain-Jane with the name of some juco block lettered across the bottom.) The wrestling, to no one's surprise, is garbage. They whiff. Try moves they don't realize until it's too late that their bodies won't allow them to do. (*That'll never fly,* I think, watching a thick-gutted man try to do a half-assed attempt at a moonsault—a move that even advanced wrestlers don't sniff at unless they're supremely confident in their core strength and flying abilities—and collapse backward off the buckle.) In seconds, most are winded (should've never had that sixth beer before signing up, bud). Openmouthed breathing, heavy pulls of air (gotta put your arms over your head or double over, old man). Most in the crowd snicker or cheer. Family members or friends of the participants, probably, who promised them a free cold one for getting in the ring. I can't help myself. I'm high as God's windvane.

"Boo," I say, honestly the first time in my life I boo anything. Realize at that moment how stupid the sound is, but it comes out again, stronger the second time. "Boo! Boo!"

The act of putting my negativity into the world gives me power. I put my whole body into it, almost bounce in my seat.

A young man who is surrounded by a crowd of like-minded folks turns to me and calmly says, "Hey, man, why don't you just keep that to yourself." It's a fair demand, and he asks me in a straightforward way. (All the signs point to the asker being ex-military as he has a buzz cut and that giveaway tat of an eagle atop the globe in front of an anchor on his right forearm.)

Before I can think of an adequate comeback, it comes out. A laugh. Not even a laugh. More like a giggle. Childish. Then the dam breaks, and I'm snickering hard.

Not sure if the laughter is because of the weed in my system or because sometimes in awkward situations you have to expend emotion, and being a male (although one raised by a firebrand of a woman), I wasn't really given the tools to adequately process my feelings. And so it bubbles up as nervous laughter. Like going vocal at a funeral. This pisses everyone off more. Way more than had I actually said something insulting. Which in turn only makes me laugh harder. I'm in tears.

(The weird thing is the whole time I'm laughing, I'm thinking, *Why am I laughing?* I'm not sure what comes over me. You'd think a man raised by a woman would be better equipped to verbalize his inner limbo. Should be a genteel soul, write villanelles in my free time, but it took me until my late teens to stop macho posturing. Talking decades of weaning out the dickhead. Saving it for the ring.)

A man next to the man speaks out, "This guy is a hero; you don't know what he's sacrificed."

Buzzcut Lightweight gives a smirk and puts his head down, and I can make out a scar running along the left side of his head.

"Boo! Boo! Boo!" I scream like it's my safe word.

"Listen, sir, they're just having a go. It's all fun and games," the marine says.

"Boo!"

"Wait, I recognize this sonuvabitch," says the guy with the guy. He pulls his phone from his pocket and taps at apps, rotates, types letters into a search bar. Pulls up a video: it's me screaming for America's head. (But I get the sense it's remixed as there's some bad Middle Eastern music underneath the thing.) "This is the guy who hates this here US of A."

Some of the crowd catch on; others, who probably have no clue as to what he's talking about, are content to go with the herd. I'm booing middle-aged, beer-swilling father figures and have dismissed a marine.

The first one comes like a rifle report, pinging off a seat behind me. The rocket is a crushed-up beer can. The next one hits me dead in the neck.

Candy wrappers, ticket stubs, full sodas. Spit. It all rains down on me.

My mouth is open. I walk away.

Two men follow me, get that twitch in their hands and forearms, signs they want to scrap. They're two knuckleheads in matching camo jackets and trucker caps (who would've cheered another me, past me, almost-big-league me, not fat, disabled, grinning-dumbly me). I'm not against it, but I'm clearly at a disadvantage in my current-necked state. The military man who I started the skirmish with actually catches up to us and pulls them back, both physically and verbally. "Boys, this guy is clearly in no position," I hear him say. "Fucking cripple," one of the ham hands says. "Get the fuck out of here," the other says.

I walk off, a garbage monster with a plastic Lay's bag stuck to my heel, like a piece of toilet paper I can't shake.

Mom is hanging at the shaved-ice station. She's holding a half-chewed funnel cake on a grease-soaked paper plate. She is talking to the shaved-ice lady, who looks like she and Mom could've been old poker friends. Ice Lady has a big pouf of Kool-Aid-red hair and one-shade-less-red lipstick. They've got a shorthand like they used to watch each other's kids.

It takes Mom a second to realize I'm coated in gross. "Ricky, this here's Joyce. Joyce has devoted the last fifteen years of her life to shaved ice and traveling from carnival to state fair to Little League World Series. Isn't that something?" Mom is high, too. She has the heavy-lidded look of someone fresh-stepped from a dream. I put two and two together and figure that while I was getting blown underneath the bleachers, she met Joyce and they bonded over something else. We are in Colorado.

Then she takes another look at me. "What happened to you?"

"Give me the keys, Mom."

"Where are you going?"

"Home. I'm going home."

"Right now? You're way too loopy," she says, and twirls her finger in a circle around her head to show I'm out of my mind. She nearly drops her funnel cake.

"I can drive, Mom, now give me the keys."

"I'm too high. You're too high."

"I'll be fine."

"Remember that time in high school, sophomore year, when you first got your car and you and Yuri got so loaded that you thought the road was shrinking and you freaked out and called me to come pick you up since you knew Yuri's dad would lose his shit? And it turned out that you'd driven down a detour onto a golf path."

"I've smoked a lot since then," I say, although I mean to say "grown." Grown a lot since then. Mom pulls the keys out of her pocket, picks a broken cigarette filter free that's wedged between them, and hands them over.

She turns back to Joyce and says, "Kids." And Joyce, fucking Joyce, nods in agreement.

"Stay in your slot, Joyce," I say out loud, meaning to say it in my head. Pretty sure I spit flecks from my lower lip onto Joyce's glass.

"Excuse me?" Joyce says. She smacks her lips.

"Apologize, Ricky," Mom says.

"I'm out of here," I say, go for something big, reach through the opening, and grab one of the large syrup dispensers from in front of Joyce. But it doesn't come clean. It clangs and clunks and the top of the plastic dispenser comes off. But I finally slide the thing through. It's full of blue goo that's probably flavored like the rumor of a fruit. Joyce and Mom are so shocked they stay mum. Good luck getting it back, Joyce.

Don't think it dawns on Mom what I'm saying, or she believes I'm bluffing. Probably thinks I'm going to sit in the car and wait her out.

I should consider how Mom is going to get home, but I'm not worried about her. She once told me a story about how, pre–cell phones, she was on a spring break road trip with college girlfriends and was accidentally left at a rest stop near Abilene, Texas. Ended up hitchhiking all the way back to Lawrence. She stared at a map for too long at an entrance opposite the one they entered, and their Volkswagen bus was gone. They had thought she was asleep under a pile of blankets in the back of the bus.

She's going to figure it out. Or maybe she'll join Joyce on the road. Make a life from shaved ice and candy-colored syrups. Guilt will hit me later, of course, but for now I've got a giant jug of blue sugar syrup, the munchies, and a mission to get home.

I find the car in the parking lot that's actually a scrubbed-out field. I turn the keys in the ignition and drive straight to Omaha. Gobble up a few more weed-infused foods. Not sure if it's the CBD or anger fueling me, but I barely notice my neck as I drive. I know I'll be in hurts-to-pee pain later, but right now weed and rage are keeping me charged.

The only stops I make are to piss and grab gas. I don't even make my first stop until I'm at a rest area outside of Alma. I rinse my arms, my face, the back of my neck, my hair. I cup water in both hands and let it pour over me. Wash off the sticky soda and spit. When I leave and the next dude comes in to piss, he gives me a long look because it's an easy seventy-five-degree, sun-high-in-the-sky day, but I'm drenched like I caught a downpour under a rain cloud for one. Also, I'm still carrying the blue raspberry dispenser under my arm, half-filled, half long gone. And I'm wearing this damn brace.

When I leave, I approach a water fountain out front of the rest area and instead of going around, I walk through. Because you know who beats a straight path? An honest man, that's who. And there's no point in life when I'm more direct with myself. Me: a shit-smelling temporary cripple, not knowing what stranger's strange-smelling dick jizzed into Mom's warm pocket to produce exactly half of me, but the one thing I can be sure of is that the dude's likely white. (Which makes me white.) Thank you, Colorado, for this parting gift. You goddamned square.

CHAPTER TWENTY-TWO

JOBBERS ARE LOSERS. Their whole game is to lose. To make the name look good.

During the era I grew up in, jobbers routinely faced off against big-name wrestlers on Saturday mornings. As I got older and wrestling shifted to the Monday Night Wars and other outlets, people put up less with watching jobbers and wanted name-on-name hot branded action.

When I was a kid, it was a treat to see a name versus a name. You'd have to wait until a big event.

Growing up, Mom created this mythos around Jeremiah. He was the name. Everyone else who paraded through our lives were jobbers. But Mom thought that with no biological dad, a loner like me needed positive male reinforcement. The first guy to introduce me to wrestling was Austin. Austin was a dweeb who had no real knowledge of the WWF—excuse me, WWE—but knew it was something that young boys at the time took to like wrestlers to fanny packs. Like Austin to pleated pants. Mom trusted Austin. Looking back, she only dated him because she thought he'd be a good influence. Austin wasn't even Mom's type.

Whenever he drank anything that was colder than room temp, he'd wrap a napkin around it, even sitting in the comfort of home. And he would clear his throat every five minutes like clockwork; you could cook an egg to it. I can't imagine going through the motions of dating someone just because you thought it was in your kid's best interest, an effort to nudge him away from a life of whippets and bowie knives. Knuckle tats and black-market, bathtub-iced organs. Mom brought this dude into my life, who then brought wrestling with him. Took me to see the WWF, and we ran into Mantaur at a nearby gas station where I loaded up on junk food. Mantaur was filling up his rental car, looking pedestrian other than his weird sculpted hair and fanny pack. Whenever you saw wrestlers of that era in their street clothes, they always wore fanny packs. Was it because they weren't used to pockets? Although Austin wasn't in our lives for long—Mom couldn't keep up the facade—the fact that he brought me to my first live show, that he took the time to listen to me gab on and on about this name vs. that jobber meant the world. In our lives, Austin was a jobber. But without jobbers, the Pistol Whatleys, the Barry Horowitzes, the Brooklyn Brawlers, the stars couldn't shine. Austin was here and then he wasn't, but he always let Mom take the stage. Austin made me learn to respect the little guy, the no-name.

But not every jobber was as easygoing as Austin. The majority of them were dickheads. Dudes over the years treated me like shit, treated her like shit, or treated both of us equally shitty. They smacked me, forgot my name, locked me in my room. Or worse, did terrible things to her emotionally or physically, and I was helpless to do anything at that age.

Then there was Metal Craig. A dude who pulled a dick move. A literal dick move.

One time, when I was five, right into my early love affair with wrestling, Mom scored tickets to a WWF match at the Orpheum. At the time she was dating a guy named Craig who seemed like he might take. This was right after Austin. Mom called him Metal Craig because he loved to listen to cassette tapes of Slayer and Motörhead. Metal Craig also had a whole bottom row of fake teeth. He'd pop them out or wiggle them around in his mouth just to mess with people. He told me the originals rotted because he smoked meth, and then when he gave up meth, he gatewayed to Rocky Road.

Metal Craig wore a lot of denim and always had a hard pack of smokes, Marlboro Reds, in his front left breast pocket. Metal Craig was around, Mom told me, for about a year and a half, give or take. I loosely remember him; I mostly remember that he had long, swoopy black hair (Mom had a type) and a thin mustache that, in hindsight, I'm sure he wished were thicker. Metal Craig was decent. He wouldn't really cut my sandwiches the way I wanted (diagonal or get the fuck out), but he never did anything to wrong me. That was until Mom, he, and I went to the WWF event. I don't even really remember who wrestled. The Legion of Doom was there. The Hardy Boyz. Chris Jericho. I mostly remember it was cold and I couldn't see that well and Mom allowed me to eat a bunch of snacks and drink soda for like the third time in my life.

After downing a twenty-ounce soda, I needed to pee, and Mom asked Metal Craig to take me. He reluctantly agreed. While he wasn't really into wrestling, I remember the glitz or glamour or the production value (or maybe the hot ringside managers) piqued his interest. He didn't want to come with me, but he did. The bathroom was old-school: no separate urinals, only a single long trough. There weren't that many people in the bathroom as the action was going. As a child, I could barely sidle up to the trough. I did the little-kid thing of dropping my pants all the way to the ground, ass fully exposed.

Metal Craig cowboyed up next to me, wide-stanced like riding a horse. Unfurled his giant dick. It looked like the snout of a monster I'd seen on a sci-fi movie poster. Veiny and thick. His stream shot out all powerful and ropy.

I looked around everywhere and anywhere but directly at it.

He looked down at me and I freaked out in my little-kid brain and screamed, "Don't look at my pee-pee!"

"You afraid?" he said, chortled.

Spritzed me a little. On purpose. Like when you're watering the lawn or washing the car and you thumb the nozzle of the garden hose to get the wide spray. He did that with his dick. Finger over the peehole. Angled at my face.

Definitely wet my lips. For the record, piss tastes terrible. Don't let anyone fool you. That's why on those strange addiction shows where pregnant women eat chalk or hoard old cat hair to reshape in the image of their long-dead tabby, the weirdo who shows up and feigns interest in drinking his own piss always looks like a vampire and can barely get it down. Slowly sips it in front of the camera. Secret's out: piss tastes fucking terrible.

All my life, Mom paraded through a series of jobbers. Good to bad, most leaned scumbag. Most were forgettable, except Austin and Metal Craig. But there were always the stories about Dad.

Dad, the marquee name. Dad, the star.

Now it turns out my biological father might be a part-time yogi, which, by default, makes him a jobber. Meaning I'm a jobber. The son of a jobber is a jobber, and his bloodline is destined to be nothing but jobbers. Jobbers and piss-lippers up and down the line.

CHAPTER TWENTY-THREE

HOME, I CRASH. Fatigue gets me into a figure-four leg lock, and it doesn't even let me do my usual careful do-si-do into the best possible bed-ready prone position. My body crumples into itself and I'm dragging ass before I lights-out. After a few hours of shut-eye, waking up groggy and not remembering where I am, a stench of dry spit overpowering from a puddle of it pooled on my pillow, I remember everything. Wake, smoke, shower. Pop a few pills to blunt the ache from five hundred miles on my spine.

I grab some of my belongings, mostly what's already in the back of my car, and throw in a few records, books, movies, and clothes into a hamper and take off. I can no longer live at Mom's.

"Amigo, you have to believe me, I never expected it to be that gnarly. I didn't think you'd actually get hurt," Johnny says on the other end of the line. Good old America with the empty promises. I don't actually care whether or not he's telling the truth, I need a place to stay and figure I can guilt him into giving me a couch to sleep on for a few weeks. "Donnie told me not to tell you because those kinds of switches have to look real. If you knew, maybe you wouldn't sell it. I didn't think I'd make contact that hard."

I don't even pay attention to what he's saying; it all drones on, like your roommate's PowerPoint presentation on why to buy a chiminea.

"Look, I forgive you, man," I say.

"Really?"

"Yeah," I say, although I'm not sure if I completely do, but beggars and choosers. He doesn't say anything back for a sec. Maybe the moment is too sincere. I play it like the line went fuzzy.

"Anyway, water under the bridge, pal."

"Definitely. Also, hate to ask, but . . ."

Johnny lives in a fixer-upper in Gifford Park. The kind of boring, flat gray, everyday home I wish were haunted so at least it'd have some character. Best it has to offer is a lot of spiderwebs, which isn't close enough. Johnny says "craftsman bungalow," as if those words mean anything to me. Three barely trees that don't grow shit and offer zero shade take up real estate in the front yard. The "bungalow" sits next to a soccer field that they use for neighborhood meet-and-greets and farmer's markets. I sleep in the garage. Catch dust on a duvet with three pillows, which doesn't quite meet my needs, but I'll have to make do. I also snagged an afghan Mom made for me when I first hit the road to wrestle. Johnny and I are the type of household that look like we're perpetually moving in. Furnishings are bare minimum: six total shared DVDs, three spoons, a framed photo of Goldberg over the mantel. A refrigerator box turned on its side as a dining table.

Over the next few weeks, we build an easygoing rapport: I do dishes, he cooks or buys takeout or gets delivery pizza. We have beers after Johnny gets back from work at his Costco job. He does quick-hit Photoshop jobs, a skill he picked up in high school. He fixes old scratches and makes color corrections, but sometimes when he's bored he'll also make a second copy where he tints everyone's faces green and calls it Masking. "Like *The Mask*," Johnny says. "Somebody stop me!"

I still have a few more weeks in my current braced state. So during the day, to not be a complete hermit, I go to Blue Line, a small coffee shop in Dundee, and flirt with the barista, who once showed me her antique watch. I had wanted to propose while I held her wrist.

Mom calls, but eventually, after I let the seventh one go to voice mail, she stops. Knows I'll reach out when I'm ready. She does hit me with the info that one Roy Templeton is a resident of Green Bank, West Virginia. Sure she's giving it up as a peace offering.

Johnny keeps me looped into the world of semipro wrestling, Pro Mag and other tours included. Part of me doesn't want to know, and the other part tells him to keep going, like a jilted lover stumbling across an ex's cam show. Bojorquez is no longer champion. He'd actually been called up to NXT, the WWE's development league. I thought I'd heard something about this, but since the injury, I'd stopped reading all the blogs, watching all the YouTube videos, washing dishes to all the podcasts. Johnny thought he was the next man up, but his popularity has remained stagnant, and there is a new kid, El Guapo.

Johnny once, at home, while showing me El Guapo's moves, mutters under his breath, "Fucking Mexicans." How appropriate, America, how appropriate. He isn't so much a racist as a man who let his paranoia lead him to the shores of racism. He feels like he's being undermined by a group of people, but really it's one man who became The Man who has superior skills to Johnny; only that one man is a card-carrying member of the same group as The Man before him. But also, Johnny is probably racist. El Guapo isn't as good as Bojorquez, but he has great ring generalship. He plays to the crowd. Does a move with a mirror and slicking back his hair with a comb. Throws the comb into the stands and even the most hard-hearted trolls cheer.

"Cheer up," I say to Johnny. Give him a mouse pad I bought him. "Let's hit the courts," I say to try and take his mind off wrestling. If he lets that sickness bleed into his brain, he's going to go fully alt-right, get his hair cut in that undercut style and talk about "gospel" when he's mentioning message boards. He already has the German lineage.

We play outdoor volleyball on sand courts right next to Schrempf's. Well, Johnny does, and I sit on the benches and drink. Marfa is a new server. Not an on-the-court corner-to-corner sizzler. Not even a high-loft underhander. She serves me Coronas with limes and watches me watch Johnny go spike crazy.

She approaches and sets a Bud down in front of me. "Nice neck brace," she says.

"Cervical collar."

"You'd like to do what to my what?"

"I didn't order a Bud."

"On the house," she says, winks.

"But I ordered a Corona."

Marfa tells me she's not named after the town in Texas. She says she was meant to be named Martha, but her mom had a loopy scrawl, and her parents thought it was funnier to keep it that way. She says, on the contrary, they weren't bad parents, but they were so-rich-we-don't-care parents. Threw cash at any problem. Even problems that cash couldn't solve. Paid a teenage neighbor to explain the menstrual cycle to her. She's telling me all this thirty minutes after we meet. As we're quickly undressing each other in the women's restroom at Schrempf's.

Marfa has a lean body; there are hints of abs, and she's really tan. She also has a C-section scar and the word GENIUS tattooed across her almost-abs. Another tattoo of a switchblade across her wrist. Her plum-colored lipstick is smeared across my face.

We get lewd in the restroom. I go to town with my mouth, which is pretty painful as I'm crouched down and she's grabbing my collar forcefully. Like gripping one of those steering wheels in a family-size whitewater raft amusement ride; more for stability and less to steer. Afterward, she gives me a sloppy hand job. The women's restroom at Schrempf's might be the most photographed bathroom in Omaha. So many women have taken Instagram photos pissing on the pot. The walls are a pastel-pink tile and have graffiti all over them. Screams punk, but in a millennial pink. Weird, because having seen it on my feed, I feel like I know the place well, down to the placement of every sticker on the mirror, regardless of having never been inside before. Like visiting a holy shrine or a tourist hot spot. I don't know. I'm in there for fifteen minutes, tops, giving and receiving all while trying to keep it down. Or rather, keep it up while keeping it down.

Marfa is bad news. I know this going in, but there are times you wade into deep waters for the thrill of it. If dating Frankie Rae was exciting and new, like getting one of those fad pedicures where tiny fish nip at your dead toe skin, Marfa is like the same pedicure, but instead of dipping into fish, your toes are thrust into fresh-edged Legos and mini-figs holding tridents.

Within an hour of meeting Marfa, she tells me that she's on the run from her psycho ex-boyfriend in South Dakota. He's such a space cadet that he stashed twenty thousand dollars' worth of drug funds in his apartment and then, she tells me and crosses her heart, he got so high that he forgot. She tells me he does all the drugs. Meth, coke, you name it. New airplane fuel shit they're doing in Russia. Krokodil's next of kin. So, because she wasn't really in love with him anyway, she grabbed a bunch of his drugs, his money, and her kid, and vamoosed to Omaha.

She doesn't know anyone here, but it was a big enough city within a decent day's drive.

Can't tell if she's lying, but she shows me a duffel bag full of mushrooms and tells me to take a handful. "Dig in," she says, like I'm a kid in front of a candy jar.

The third night we hang out, I don't have a condom, but she says it's all right. And the whole time she keeps saying, "Don't come, don't do it, don't do it." Like a wimpy kid warning me not to touch what appears to be a dead snake. Joke's on her, because the only thing I'm laser-focused on is how much searing pain is working its way from my neck through my spine (no matter how upright I try to keep my posture), which is a natural hard-dick deterrent.

Her kid is a weirdo, but I have empathy for him. His name's Townes because she loves Townes Van Zandt, but I think it's a bit morbid to name your kid after a drug addict no matter how good his croon. She says she almost named him Ray after Ray LaMontagne. "You should've called him LaMontagne, like a musketeer," I say. "Cuz this motherfucker brought a sword to a gunfight." I proceed to no-scope his ass in *COD*; it's the first time we're really hanging out. He gets upset and throws down his controller.

He has a bowl haircut and smells like a sneeze. He has a tiny lizard that he handles all day.

"Nice gecko," I say.

"It's a Chinese water dragon," he says.

I want to say, *Fuck you, there's no way you knew that until you read it off a sign at the pet store, you mouthy shit,* but I just say, "Cool. He doesn't look Chinese."

I try to bond with Townes. We're in Johnny's kitchen. Townes is hunched over an island in the middle of the room. I'm sitting at this secondhand dining table Johnny found at an antique shop. Chunky, dark wood piece that's far too nice for our not furnished home. Like something out of *Game of Thrones*. It's late afternoon, and Townes is eating stale cereal and I'm feasting on potatoes and sausage. The only things other than oven pizzas that I can afford. I offer to take Townes to a movie. Lego Brand Deal. Float the idea. Show I'm trying. Marfa is watching us from the living room. They're over three nights a week, since her apartment is in a sketchy part of South O. I used to live over there, and once I dragged a dresser to the street and in the two minutes it took me to check my mail, walk back upstairs, and enter my third-floor apartment, I looked out the window to see a man struggling to heft it into the trunk of his old Accord. Marfa only even receives her mail every other day. She's leafing through a *People* magazine she lifted from a neighbor's mailbox.

"So, what do you think, Townes?" I ask.

"Maybe."

"I'll stop you right there," Marfa says. "You're not going."

"What?" I skewer a chunk of roasted potato with my knife. Pop it into my mouth.

"Stop trying the dad thing. You're not his dad. You'll never be his dad. So don't try."

"I wasn't—"

"Yeah," Townes pipes up. On the regular, this motherfucker's as lonesome dove as a lighthouse keeper, but the second his mom speaks up, he's suddenly bold as a superhero.

His mom's confidence has him going.

"Yeah," Marfa says.

"Yeah," Townes says. They're getting louder and louder. Chanting it now. Townes goes over to her and they're holding hands, yelling, "Ring Around the Rosie"–ing my ass.

I mean to grab Townes by his shoulders to get him to stop, but as soon as I reach out for him, since kids are slick as parking-lot oil spills, he immediately shoots underneath my grasp and runs in the opposite direction. Only he slips on his mom's pilfered *People* and flies into the air before landing on his back.

I want to scream in his face, *Right on, you little bitch. Go cry to your mommy, you bowl-headed dipshit.* But in reality, I put on my best sad face and feign concern. My voice goes a little high. "Oh, Townes, are you okay? Are you okay, buddy?" I reach over to stand him up, but he flinches like I was the one who destroyed his Lego Death Star.

Marfa yells at me, "Don't touch him." And so I leave even though it's where I live. I go to a bar for a few drinks even though it's only three in the afternoon and hope that they're not there when I get back. I can't stand being in that dreary-ass sunken setting for too long, so I hoof it to Walmart. Walk those aisles for a solid hour. Consider buying another three-pack of white T-shirts that are identical to the six white ones I have at home.

When I return home, three hours later, I hear two adults chatting in the living room. Like they're about to spring a surprise party.

"Sounds like something he'd do," Johnny says.

"He's called Townes a dipshit before," Marfa says.

Johnny's voice gets softer. "Yeah, he's bumming off me a little too much. I mean, I'm sorry about the dead end with your dad or whatever, but try to get a job, man. Help out more around the house."

I step into the room loudly. I step so that my leg almost extends at a ninety-degree angle. Sharp like a goddamned North Korean soldier marching to celebrate Supreme Leader. My elbow almost catches and tips over a lamp. I make a noise with my throat that's supposed to be a cough but comes out a quick choke.

Marfa's eyes do that narrowed, throwing-daggers thing, but they're less knives and more baseball bats to the circumstance. Johnny says, "Hey, man, just get home?" I swear they were just holding hands.

CHAPTER TWENTY-FOUR

JOHNNY DRAGS ME to Yardbirds. Scene of so many crimes. We aren't going to solve anything right then and there, so better for the two dudes to exit the premises and let Marfa giddyup at her own pace. It's been close to five months since I last had a drink there. The owners, Rhonda and her husband, Skinny George, are behind the bar, as usual. Rhonda is five foot wind, but she has incredible forearm strength and will arm wrestle any dude within twenty pounds of her and, more often than not, win; Skinny George used to have all this Nazi iconography needled onto his arms, but since finding Rhonda he had it covered up with black sleeves that stretch from wrist to shoulder. If you look hard enough, you can make out the tip of a Third Reich visor creeping out around his armpit. People play pool on the new red felt. The bar replaced it recently, and right before they ditched the worn green stuff, patrons marked it up with Sharpied dicks and slurs. A few stand around waiting for their turn at darts. I need to scoot by them, temporarily stop the game as I take money out of my account since it's cash-only.

Skinny George yells at me, "Machine's broken."

I say, "Works for me," and hope that it actually does—otherwise I look dumb as fuck and put this dart game on hold for zip. It's an old ATM with a green screen and buttons that don't even align with the arrow prompts, but it still whirs and grinds, and where I'm expecting a couple of nicely lined-up fives is a whole lot of nothing. I apologize to the dart throwers and have to ask Johnny to front me. Skinny George shakes his head.

Johnny and I drink, our heads downturned. Him, brooding, because he isn't yet making the leap he expected to make in wrestling. Me, down and out because no dad, Mom gone, I'm in a neck brace, life in general is shit. We line up tallboy after tallboy of Bud like we're about to take back porch target practice with his Airsoft. I thumb apart the layers of a wet cardboard coaster.

"Listen, Ricky," Johnny says. And gives a sigh like he's about to launch into something serious, but I keep putting beer after beer and shot after shot in front of him to keep him distracted.

"Nice cervical collar," someone behind me says. A Southern lilt in her voice.

I spin on my stool and see Frankie; she beams at me. Yardbirds has dim lighting, it feels like the entire place is underwater, so she has to walk by one of the few lights in the place before I get a good look at her. Her hair is buzzed on one side and then fluffs out on the other, shows off half her beautiful skull. A helluva head shape. She has on dark red lipstick and an oversized dad sweatshirt over a vintage blue dress. She's wearing dirty white Keds, her go-to shoe, and she looks light on her feet, but when she stomps I can feel it in my jaw.

She comes up to me and holds her arms out for a hug. When we go for it, I bump my slight pooch off hers. "I haven't been moving much," I say. Hers, it dawns on me, is a baby bulge.

"Yeah, this," she says. "Five months."

Times, you feel so cheap-shotted by life, you want to run away, cuddle up into the warmest down comforter you have and lie in bed so long you feel like you'd sink into it far enough to get sucked into another dimension. Where pain doesn't exist and donuts are a form of currency. I almost feel tears so deep that they start at the back of my throat. I want to push her and Johnny over while clotheslining my arm across the bar, knocking everything over. Napkins and straws and lime wedges everywhere. She grabs me by my wrist. She still knows me.

"Listen: I'm sorry. Not just for this," she says, gesturing at her belly. "But for everything. Everything you're going through. Even if I don't know the details, I can see it in your face. But just know that this isn't about you, Ricky. It wasn't like I made a choice to pick him over you. I'm at a better place in my life. I decided I could do this."

She holds my hand in her hand. Looks me in the eyes without blinking.

"I'm sure that doesn't make you feel any better, but I promise I still have love for you, and this isn't about you and me. It's about me," Frankie says.

Even though everything she's saying feels heartfelt and meant to do as little damage to me as possible, it still hits like a knee to my heart's groin. But the kind of knee I need, especially right now.

I stand there, not saying a word, but after years of mashing bods together, you get to know someone in intimate, unspeakable ways. She knows I need air. She asks, "Cig?" And I nod yes, and just like that, her hand still in my hand, we walk outside to the smoking bench right outside the front door. She leads, and I follow, apprehensive, like a first-timer going through a haunted house. The neon signs advertising beer and pool blink above us.

"I look great, I know," Frankie says, fluffing the hair on one side of her head, laughing. "How've you been, though? How's Mom?" she asks.

I tell her Mom revealed to me that the dude I thought was the dude all these years is probably not the dude. That the woman who would've been my grandma took one look at me and basically said, *Fuck off. Not a chance.* I cut out the part about the attempted incest orgy and leaving Mom in the lurch. I throw in a few details, but only the ones that don't leave me looking like complete trash. Hard to play these things to your ex. Show her that my life is shit, so she feels a little bad for me? Or throw my arms in the air, all jubilant, to show her I've moved on? I don't do either, because Frankie knows me too well.

"So, how you doing, Frankie? Who's the lucky guy?" I light a Red, but it's a 100. The gas station attendant must not have been a smoker and passed it into the bag while I wasn't paying attention. Nobody smokes 100s unless you're an elegant lady. Frankie gives me a look. I know she wants a hit, so I pass it to her without saying a word.

"His name's Eric." Her face looks questioning. She either doesn't want me to know the truth about Eamon or can't bring herself to say his name to my face. I don't blame her. I can barely say it without cracking a grin. Definitely not marquee-worthy.

"How'd you meet?" I ask, like I don't know shit about the guy. I know the moles on his face and the faint birthmark on his left cheek. I know he loves Guy Fieri flagship restaurants. I know he could never love her as much as I did. Do.

"We met after an improv class," she says, passes me back the thin cig.

I give her a look like a sitcom dad disappointed in finding his daughter's stash. Hurt.

"Oh, wait, that was you," she says, laughs. "I'm kidding, Ricky. I'm joking."

"Brutal," I say, like I don't mean it, but I mean it.

"We met at work."

I give her another look. Scope the new buzz.

"This?" she asks, noticing me noticing her head. "I was going a little stir-crazy."

Frankie pulls off her sweatshirt. Her dress makes her look like she could be on the cover of an old country album if she were holding a rooster in a field. She bunches up the sweatshirt in her lap. We pass the cig back and forth.

"Listen, Mr. West Virginia might be your dad. Why not track him down? You've already gone so far, why pull up right before the finish line? You don't want to go another five or ten years without knowing. What if he's no longer around?"

"Why would you say that?"

"You never know. But seriously, don't wake up in a few years and pull yourself off a friend's couch and wonder what happened to Daddy and it turns out he died in a logging accident a week before. Then you'll really be insufferable."

"Really know how to dig in the heel when you're kicking a man on the ground."

"This thing almost off?" she asks, and runs her fingers daintily across the back of my neck. Puts her fingers to her nose. "Smells."

"What would Eric say about this?"

"We're not married yet. And besides, if the kid comes out a few IQ points shorter, I'll tell her to seek you out for advice on living a pretty full life regardless of being such a dumbass."

"I hate you."

"You love me."

"I know."

We're hunched close on the bench. Our hands touch again, and we let them linger there for a minute. A crew of business-casual, twenty-something dudes file by, ready to begin their big night out. A motorcycle revs down the street, bringing us to attention. "I'm going to go inside," Frankie says. "Thanks for the smoke."

"It was good seeing you, Frankie," I say.

"I know," she says, ducks inside.

I take one final drag off the cig, the last place our lips met. I sit in the still night, wanting the moment to go on even though it's already over. I want to empty out the blood bank.

CHAPTER TWENTY-FIVE

IT'S ALL ABOUT the angles and keeping it wet. Rhythm. Patience. You'll never get the right edge by rushing it.

Sharpening knives, that is. It's a cheap hobby and gives me something to do while working my upper body. I stockpile old sterling silver that dead grandparents bequeathed to couldn't-care-less grandchildren who then unloaded them on thrift stores or at estate sales. Benson has five thrift spots on the main strip, and any of them will have bins of dropped-off silver. Sets will go for a few bucks, easy.

I only need a waterstone, paper towels, toothbrushes, rubbing alcohol, sponges, rust remover, and lube. It all costs me less than fifty dollars, and I have a new hobby to take up my time.

I watch one hundred–plus hours of YouTube videos. Learn about knife angularity. How "whet" is a verb.

I'm in my bedroom with a basin of water rubbing and scraping and cleaning. I'm turning old butter knives into steak knives. By changing the angles.

Johnny will get back from work, and I'll step out of the garage sopping with sweat and dirty water. Give him a "hey." Then I'll go back into my room and he'll hear the rhythmic swish-swish for hours.

I had this same crazy focus as a kid. I watched *The Mighty Ducks* and got hockey obsessed. Spent a whole summer on rollerblades trying to perfect the knuckle puck before realizing it was cinematic magic. Rocked a blue bandana with rough-cut eyeholes and a wooden sword to ninjutsu a neighbor kid after watching *Ninja Turtles*. Eventually, every craze fell by the wayside. Wrestling was the only thing to click.

Soon, we have drawers and drawers full of flatware. Johnny asks me, "Hey, partner, can you cool it with the knife thing?"

"Sure," I say, and as he walks away I pretend he's prancing on a knifepoint. When he bends over before he leaves the room, I use perspective to pretend I'm poking him in the butt. "Poke, poke," I say to myself.

I realize I'm doing it just to be doing it. And then it loses its luster. You know how people act like being a die-hard movie buff fronts as a personality? Or they use odd passions as stand-ins? Like the weirdo at camp who's asked about his home life and answers by flicking on a lighter to watch the flame dance. Only, I've got knives. One day I look around and see them lined up in my room. Crammed in drawers. Stacked in cabinets. All that old silver, given a new edge. But me, I'm still the same weak-necked motherfucker. Only dirty and wet. And surrounded by a stupid amount of knives.

CHAPTER TWENTY-SIX

TODAY IS THE day. Hairdo says, "Today's the day." He looks me in the eyes and I almost blush. I have to stare at the pocked ceiling. Eye the informational posters about coughing into my elbow crook, vampire-style.

"Indeed, Doc," I say. "I'll almost miss her."

"Bronze it if you get nostalgic," he says. Then it sounds like he calls me a bitch under his breath.

"What?" I ask.

"Nothing," he says. A nurse in blue scrubs stifles a laugh.

When it comes off, I feel a little stiff, but there's a freedom that makes me want to find a mountaintop, or at the very least a hillock, and scream from the top. I reach back to feel the scars, and Hairdo slaps my hand away.

He gives me the rundown about immediate life postcollar. Says the bones will continue to get stronger for up to a year.

"Maintain safe lifting techniques. Keep up a protein-rich diet. Avoid smoking."

"What about sex?" I ask. When I was wrestling, I knew who I was. When I got hurt, I retreated. Used the neckwear as a defense against physical and emotional intimacy. Fell into a few affairs, but almost by accident, like a cartoon character slipping into an open manhole, only I was getting swallowed up by vagina.

"Sure," he says.

"'Sure' as in 'okay'? Do I have to make any changes?"

"'Sure' as in *Sure, you're having sex.* Did you say you've been having sex?"

"Yeah, but not like a lot. Also I felt safer with the brace. Protection."

"Yeah, okay, some lady gave you the business. She ride you with her hands holding the collar?" He makes a motion like grabbing the saddle while riding a bucking bronc.

"Doesn't this go against hippo rules?"

"What?"

"Being a dickhead."

"I get paid either way."

I cough into the open air.

CHAPTER TWENTY-SEVEN

BODIES ARE REAL bastards. Doesn't matter if you've been a well-greased machine. I was always an active kid. Scaled jungle gyms when my grip strength should've given out. Bounced around from couch to couch. Elders called me Wildman Ricky. I tumbled down a flight of stairs twice before the age of five. I was always high rev. But this body I'm in now doesn't feel like me.

I sit here and slap at my gut. Feel it jiggle.

Now, without the neck brace to use as a mental crutch, I have no excuses. If I ever felt eyes judging my physical appearance or gross clothes, I knew my neck brace could help deflect. Now I don't even have that shield. Have to deal with reality. I stare in the mirror, see folds and flaps.

When I first gained weight, I still had leftover stamina from my twenty-plus years of wind sprints, leg lifts, and ring cardio. You train for that long and even the hiccups only make you work harder. But at this point I've been in this body for months.

I'm not a naturally depressed person. I lucked out of getting that mix of chemical brain juice and bad circumstances to really dive into the deep end. I mean, I get sad as the next person, but the can't-get-out-of-bed-to-brush-my-teeth-making-me-question-my-existence-in-the-deep-recesses-of-my-brain has never happened to me. But while Mom and I have always been pretty open and honest, I still kept shit to myself, still brooded, was moody. Especially as a preteen. I escaped into wrestling, smoking weed, and hanging out with Yuri. Without wrestling or Mom or Frankie, when heavyweight shit hits me now, I'm not equipped with the machinery of how to deal.

Point is, all I've been doing is crying. Crying. Crying.

Feels like whatever liquid isn't making its way out of the front snake or sweat glands is finding its way out of the corners of my eyes. Because I haven't cried like this since I was a child.

One night I'm lying in bed and sense the waterworks. I just let go. Feel one drop. Then another. Bingeing classic Hanks. *Joe Versus the Volcano. Sleepless in Seattle. You've Got Mail.*

And I've never felt this free in my life. It's a release pent up for almost twenty years. Since I never had a dad, no single dude ever put that pressure on me of not showing vulnerability, but you get the general vibe from society.

So I start letting myself cry. And much like a preteen boy suddenly figuring out masturbation, once you squeeze the toothpaste out, you've got to clean your teeth with it. Kidding, of course. Point is, you can't go back.

Marfa calls me. Things have definitely cooled, but a little flame still burns. Dealing with women, I'm surprised any of them will give me the time of day, I'm feeling so damn shitty about my body. Which, poor me, right? We all know how hard it is for the other half, but try to consider the bigger picture when you've mistakenly poured water into your cereal. For the first few months, I still had the stupid swagger. The quarterback past his prime who tries to throw a tight spiral but duffs it into the dust. When so much has been built upon this empty shrine, it's hard to adapt.

But now the brace is gone. It's me and this body, and I know it's not going to last forever, but right now it feels like all I've got. I have to get out of my own head. I call Marfa.

She comes over, smelling like weed and liquor. "Great," she says, when she notices all the knives. "Please don't murder me." We both laugh, but hers is more nervous. With little preproduction, we undress in my bed and mess around. She throws most of my pillows to the ground. Bad sign, but I need this. She's putting me in her mouth and looking at me coyly with her droopy eyes. Unfortunately, I can't rise to the occasion. I use my tongue and fingers to get her off. She tries again with me, but it's no use. Might as well be slapping around a Pillsbury dough log, as soft as it is. The more she plays with it, the worse it gets. Finally, we lie back and stare at my ceiling, which is a bunch of beams. She snatches the remote and flips on the TV.

"Were you watching *You've Got Mail*?" Marfa asks. She hits play so we have background chatter.

"Been a minute."

"I've been busy. Oh, yeah, I wanted to tell you that Johnny offered to let me move in."

"America?"

"What other common Johnny? Since you're not really paying rent, he could use some help, and it'd be a nice fit. Townes got used to having more space, and you know my apartment complex isn't the safest place for either of us. It kind of works out."

I turn my back to her. We're both quiet. Hanks waxes about big business in the book industry. And without realizing it, I begin crying. Quiet at first, but then they start ripping through me; it's a real duct-clearing, body-wracking sob fest.

"Jesus, are you crying?" I can hear the disgust in her voice. "Didn't your dad ever tell you a man shouldn't cry in front of a woman?"

I guess I never got far enough with Marfa to tell her the whole truth of it. But she's right. Maybe I need to see my dad. This is two people in as many weeks telling me so.

"Please leave," I whisper. If Frankie were here, she'd be rubbing my back in wide, clockwise circles. Telling me I'd be all right.

"I can't hear you," Marfa says. "Speak up." She's holding the remote and turns the volume up on Tom. She slaps at my dick, but not in a harmful way, more like how you'd swat at a gnat or shoo a child.

CHAPTER TWENTY-EIGHT

THIS TRIP IS need-to-know only, meaning at most Johnny, so he doesn't wonder where I am when my ass indent on the couch slowly springs back. For where-the-fuck-is-Ricky purposes. Mom and I still aren't on speaking terms. We text an occasional short burst of necessary info. But then I tell Mom as soon as I make up my mind.

going to WV 2 see roy, I text. Out of the blue after a few weeks of barely anything. But I know she'll respond. Mom always responds.

Drive safe. Call me as soon as you get back.

i will

Love you, Ricky.

I need some scratch to make the trip, and I have no belongings worth pawning off. I've heard about medical experiments that will pump you full of morphine or who knows what, put you on an inhibitor, and then make you eat and sleep on a regular schedule to see how long it takes for the junk to pass through your blood. I consider it, but counting paperwork and turnaround time, it doesn't add up.

I'm getting desperate. Feels like if I don't make a move soon, maybe I never will. It's been a week and a half since I shucked the brace. It's been almost a month since I talked to Frankie. Johnny walks in from work, sets down a thermos, and asks if I can take out the trash. The can is overflowing. Coffee filter with old grounds. Empty cereal box. Orange peels. I've been too busy eating sweet corn. I'm sitting in the living room, and I can barely make out the top of the mountain from where I'm at, at least twenty feet away.

"Sure, I could do that," I say, "but what about if I make this from where I'm at and you take it out instead?"

"Ricky, I'm tired. I just want to sit down and not see my trash can overflowing."

"I mean, if you're not up for a bet, you're not up for a bet."

"Please just take it out."

"I could do that. Or if I chuck this and have it land clean, you could take it out." I'm holding a corncob and pretending to play it like a piccolo.

"Fuck. All right."

I toss the cob with the most graceful of underhanded flicks. They say, statistically speaking, more basketball players would have higher free-throw percentages if they shot underhanded, granny-style, but that shit isn't cool; went out with canvas shoes and high shorts. I have no such qualms. It lands perfectly atop a handful of wet spaghetti and a half-crushed cardboard takeout container. Then it rolls off. Lands right next to the trash can.

"Okay, happy?" Johnny asks.

"Okay, but what about double or nothing?"

"What's double taking out the trash?"

"Let's put some money on the line," I say, eyeing a deflated volleyball half-hidden behind old books. One in a million how it teeters and rocks and finds its resting place, ultimately winning me my way.

CHAPTER TWENTY-NINE

RITUAL IS WEIRD. We cling to it out of habit. Fear. Luck.

I didn't grow up sipping the God juice, but you can't cast a stone in Omaha without hitting a bank or a church, so it's part of the Midwestern existence to catch some of the splash-back of the Holy Spirit; even if you aren't religious, odds are almost all your neighbors are. Sit in a Runza and nearly all the old-timers will clasp hands and say grace before devouring their meal. Makes sense; we're the belly above the Bible Belt.

I even attended Catholic school for my first five years. It was where all the neighborhood poor kids went. My first- and second-grade teachers were actual nuns. Slap-your-hand-with-a-ruler types. The older third graders helped us memorize our prayers by saying them with us, but I never gave in. They told me I had to recite them from memory to get baptized, and I said, "No, ma'am," and sat in the back pews while the rest of the kids got their foreheads wet.

I'm not religious, but when we all cross big moments, we revert back to our programming. I still say prayers and do the stations of the cross. What's a prayer, anyways, but words on the air? I say them out of habit and in times of fear and luck.

This is all a ramble to say, when I'm headed on my way, I drive by the glass church and feel the need to enter.

The glass church is actually called Holy Family Shrine, according to the official literature. It's a giant glass-and-wood structure that's visible from both sides of I-80. It sits atop a hill and catches the light in a way that makes you believe in a higher power. I've driven by it a thousand times but never felt the call to get closer. Not until today.

Due to recent construction, I have to park over a mile away and then hike to the top of the hill. When I approach, I notice the hand-laid stones that make up the walkway to the shrine: patterns cut into the rocks reveal a running stream that works its way underneath the chapel. The entranceway that you pass through is forged into the hillside. Nature and man-made, tag team.

When I first step inside, a quiet young man with a tie on hands me a pamphlet that states the rules. No professional photography. Especially no drones. Dress attire needs to be respectful. I was actually wearing a cutoff Motörhead T-shirt, but pulled on a Huskers hoodie right before I walked in because of the windchill. Dude must be a fan, because he waves me on.

The shrine or cathedral itself isn't that long, though it's tall, with these crosshatched wood patterns that hold the glass and bounce back all that light. I hear the trickle of the stream work its way under the stone and see how they've cut it to work with the church.

It's quiet inside. Smells like earth. Looking down at the humps of grassland broken up by gray strips of highway makes me feel at ease. Certain times of the year, all that grass will get fried a dull yellow, but right now it's a dark green and a different shade of green. Clusters of cottonwoods also line the horizon. The real sight is the sky. Big blue. I feel a little more lifted, somehow, and it almost overwhelms me.

The only sound is the stream of water underfoot. The man coughs. I want to ask for a blessing, but it feels insincere in the moment. Maybe it's enough I made it up here. Giddy in all this glass, I want a sign that I'm making the right move. I want to feel high on heaven vapors, or see a manifestation of yes in thumbs up–shaped cumulus clouds or a West Virginia–specific outline in flattened prairie grass.

I take a seat. Breathe. Wait.

Hear only water. Look and see the overseer scrolling on his phone. Is this the sign? Indifference?

I feel less set on driving all the way to West Virginia, pedal mashed to the floorboard. Something in me drops. I have to turn back.

Right before I walk out, I scream, "Hallelujah!" And immediately sprint back to my car. It's the first time I've run without my neckpiece on, and I feel so damn free I might as well be a stallion breaking loose across the plains. Wind in my hair and American soil beneath me. So, naturally, I lose my nerve and hightail it home.

CHAPTER THIRTY

CRISSCROSS THIS COUNTRY enough and what will baffle you is how hard we try to make it all the same. I mean there's the individual beauty of Montana mountains or Pittsburgh bridges or Arkansas rivers. But on the outskirts, we try to flatten that feel. It's always a Motel 6, a Walmart, a McDonald's. Repeat.

Could be there's something sacred in this feeling of familiarity. Like an old T-shirt, but one that's available no matter whose dresser you peer in.

I'm in Omaha, no more than ten minutes from home. But this feels like every highway pit stop. And every highway pit stop feels like this.

I'm people watching under the fuzzed-out sodium lights of a Walmart parking lot, the world's best reality show. Curler-haired mothers in flip-flops and Mickey Mouse sweatshirts cart vats of cheese and five-dollar DVDs to their minivans. Preteens with suspenders over their basketball jerseys are hugged up on one another, backs up against Hondas with aftermarket mufflers. Also Walmart doesn't typically kick people from their parking lot, so you see RVs posted up long term.

Walmart gets a bad rap, and it certainly deserves it. Mom worked for them for a sec, and she hated it. Terrible hours, low pay, no real perks. She had an assistant manager who tried to cop a feel. She was only there for two months, but she still remembers it with disdain.

But on the consumer side, I get it. You're in unfamiliar territory, and there, in the middle of nowhere, shines a twenty-four-hour beacon. *Welcome.*

Layout is always the same. Concrete gunmetal-gray floors. High ceilings that make you aware you're in a giant warehouse. Food, electronics, housewares. They sell Velcro shoes in black or gray for less than a ten-spot. That nun who was on the sidelines for Loyola during March Madness sported them.

Maybe all that time spent in church enlightens me somehow, because I'm leafing through a giant bin of cheap kids' DVDs when I think: *I'll snag one for Townes.* Not even sure what he digs, but they're on sale, and I have lingering guilt about his *People* magazine spill. I know he doesn't like me, and I can barely stand him, but it's just the circumstances. I'm a dude who shows up to bone his mom—that's it. What allegiances is he supposed to have? And I can remember being in his position. Don't know why it took me so long to realize that, but I'm going to try harder. One of us has to be the adult here. I do know he once opened up about loving anime. It was the one time he flashed his badge at bonding. What does a South Dakota kid on the lam with his mom know about Japanese cheekbones? I hear laughter and see a stuffed animal fly over the top of the aisle dividers. "Stop, stop," I hear a woman say. It's a voice I recognize.

I see another toy—a plastic tow truck—whiz overhead. It comes down and crashes into a *Star Wars* scooter display. Knocks them over. I creep toward the culprit. The voice is definitely Marfa. She's probably chiding Townes for being a little shit. I peer down one aisle, realize they're in the next one over. Maybe I'll toss something back. Catch them by surprise. But before I do, I sneak a peek around the corner and see them standing there.

Johnny and Marfa. Marfa and Johnny. Twosome only, no Townes. Johnny's got a doll in his hands and he's pretending he's going to chuck it at any instant. He's trying to play keep-away, and she's got her arms wrapped around him. They're laughing like they invented joy.

I duck back around. Feel a red-hot pain shoot through my chest and up into my neck. While they're playing grab-ass in the toy aisle, I have to get home. Gotta beat them both back, grab my shit, and go, because I couldn't bear sitting through pretending I didn't see what I just saw. I fling the DVD I'm holding as hard as I can, and it catches flight, soars toward the ceiling, and I pray it boomerangs back to crack that two-timing America in his fucking neck. But I take off running before I can witness any physics-breaking redemptive arc.

CHAPTER THIRTY-ONE

I FLY HOME. Townes is sitting on the couch, his eyes half–glazed over from needing sleep. He's watching late-night cartoons on Adult Swim. He doesn't say a word to me.

I enter the garage. Oddly, I'm at peace. Or maybe I'm lying to myself. I grab a box and put only my most important belongings inside: documents, old trophies, a few books and DVDs. I'd already packed some essential clothes for the trip, so I put all my other ones in a trash bag. The last thing is a PS4 that Townes has coveted and probably played while I've been away, although I've warned him against handling my property.

I grab the PS4 and don't even pull the proper plugs. I just grab the plastic body. Wires dangle. Snake across the ground behind me as I walk.

I approach Townes, my things in tow. I hold the PS4 out in front of him. I've got his attention.

"Are you going somewhere?" Townes asks, rubbing his eyes. His lips are dry and crusty.

"Did you want this, Townes?" I ask.

"Yeah, why?" he asks.

Right then I drop-kick it and it shatters into a dozen-plus plastic pieces. Sony, meet foot. Small sections fly into the kitchen, ping off the island and appliances. Larger pieces skid into the living room.

"What the heck?" Townes says.

"Fuck you, Townes," I say.

Then I grab him and hold him close to my chest. I sniff his hair. "Never let your mom see you cry," I say, and then I thrust him backward.

"What?" he asks.

I toss my bags and boxes into the back seat of my car and drive to Mom's place. It's locked, and I left my key back at Johnny's and don't want to wake her at the witching hour. I get as cozy as I can on her front porch swing, use my afghan to keep warm. I love that swing. Seems like so many homes had those swings back when, but then they fell out of style. All these cookie-cutter houses out west look like they're movie sets. No real character unless you're talking about the brick facade houses in Benson or Dundee or the older "craftsman bungalows" near Hanscom. I try to fall asleep on the swing, seeing the world slowly tilt and rock. The crescent moon glows white as shit, and the stars are bright until they're not. I visit the black room.

CHAPTER THIRTY-TWO

MOM WAKES ME, and I'm curled up on the fainting couch right inside of the foyer. I have a thick red blanket on me that she's owned for at least as long as I've been alive. My shoes are off and underneath the couch. My mouth is bone-dry.

Mom hands me a large mug of coffee and a plate with bacon, eggs, and toast points rubbed in orange marmalade. I gnaw on the toast, still a bit stomach sick from subsisting on greasy fast food and gas station eats and also what I witnessed last night.

"So, what happened?" Mom asks. She sits down at this table that she lopped the end off of and now uses as a desk. She's gluing together miniature sections of a gazebo. Recently, she's been into tiny furniture and architecture. Says it helps her focus. She's actually wearing her readers, which she never likes to wear. Says they make her feel old. "Why were you left shivering on my front porch?"

"I wasn't left anywhere. I found my way here."

"Why weren't you at Johnny's?"

"I'm done there. I'm done with him."

"What happened? He hit you with another bell?" She's looking over her lenses at me.

"Too soon."

"Too soon?"

"That girl, Marfa—I saw the two of them getting cozy in the toy aisle." I spoon some runny eggs into my mouth.

"Better off. You dodged a bullet." Mom's right. Sometimes you just want a hard body. And you try to talk yourself into the good. She has pretty toes. She can utter any *Simpsons* line from the first ten seasons from memory. She likes Maiden. "What are you going to do next?"

"No clue."

"You want me to go rough her up? Give her the business?" she asks, gluing a mini-stick to another mini-stick.

"What am I five?"

"Good, because that girl does some heavy drugs, and who knows what horse tranqs she's putting down her gullet. Guarantee you wrong her and she's got juice that gives her the strength of Superwoman. On the bright side, maybe now I don't feel so bad if I call child protective services on her. Maybe the kid gets a fair shake."

"Fuck both of them," I say, pointing my spoon. A dab of egg goes air-bound.

"You know what you're doing right, Ricky? You're jumping into these quick hit-and-split relationships, because you want a warm body, which, look, I'm not judging, but it doesn't seem like you really want to be with her."

"So what do I want?" I ask, holding my mug with two hands like a child.

"Truthfully, I don't think you ever got over Frankie."

"I don't know what you're talking about."

"I can tell you this because I'm your mama. You never allowed yourself the time and space to recover from Frankie Rae. I read a study where they talked about how women typically feel the hurt of a relationship more deeply initially, but when they're over it they're over it. They grieve. Find their girlfriends. Let it all out. Men hold on to that shit and bury it, and then when they're sitting on a porch in their eighties, some bob of hair will remind them of their long-lost love, and the pain will break their hearts. And they'll keel over from grief because they never dealt with it."

"Who's Bob?"

"Sit on that. Marinate." Mom stands up and goes for an over-the-top hug. Mushes my face into her stomach. Crumbs of orange toast on her shirt get in my eyes. Which makes me tear up a touch. "Let it out," Mom says. "Let it all out."

CHAPTER THIRTY-THREE

ALTHOUGH I HAVE a vested interest in knowing about the goings-on in wrestling today, it's really tough to watch. Moves-wise, they're better than ever. Production-wise, they pour way more money into it, and it's slick as can be. Jumbotrons. Extravagant costumes. Pyrotechnics.

But all the preparation and money in the world can't make up for a lack of charisma. Can't make up for Macho Man's "Cream of the Crop" sermon. The Ultimate Warrior's hoodoo. Ric Flair's flamboyance. Macho Man did promos with trash cans. Coffee creamer. Sleight of hand with half-and-half. Rumor was he was so good he'd take bets that he couldn't make up the promo off the top with whatever was in the back room. But he always delivered.

I caught the tail end of that era. Mine was the Attitude Era headlined by Stone Cold and The Rock.

But they were the last of the riffers.

Pull up YouTube. Watch Macho Man vs. Ultimate Warrior in their Wembley Stadium promo. Nose to nose. So much fury, so much energy.

So much neon and glitter. Cowboy hats and face paint. Tassels and tighty whities. What a time to be alive.

I do catch Pro Mag every once in a while. In today's day and age, even the smaller productions film events and post them to YouTube. Facebook Live. The champ now is someone named Billy Joe Babcock. His gimmick is he wears all denim. Canadian tux. Sports a cowboy hat with no irony. Looks like the Marlboro Man, Billy Joe does. I can't believe I was so close to tasting glory.

Beat Bojorquez and who knows what path I would've been on.

Maybe I never go off the rails with Frankie. Quit the janitor gig and I'm rolling in money from being champ. Maybe even at this point, a nod from NXT or who knows, even the WWE.

Maybe I'm power walking, Vince-style, down the walkway at the CHI Health Center or Kemper Arena in KC. Mom in the crowd, Frankie and our baby wearing matching denim jackets with my name airbrushed across the back. The baby holding a sign with gibberish in crayoned scribbles.

I catch them in the crowd, give a wink and a nod. Me, I'm running, high-fiving, running, running, running, and I never stop.

CHAPTER THIRTY-FOUR

I EXPECT TO make a triumphant arrival. Like trumpets blaring from the band. High fives. High fives. High fives. Truth is, the doors barely yawn. Back at Benson High. Home court advantage.

Marjorie, hair grown out into an adult's haircut, gives me a wave from behind her glass. She points toward the principal's office. I need to pay my respects. Thank McWhorter for even allowing me the time to recover and rejoin them. Most would've axed me.

Only it's a new principal. The previous vice. I never knew her. Obviously, I saw her on occasion, but never got much face time. Vice Principal Koda beckons me into her office. Koda's nameplate has the word "Vice" covered up by a piece of masking tape colored in by marker matching the wood. Her degrees are numerous. She's a tall Japanese woman with one of those smiles that makes everyone around her smile. I can't tell if she's forty or twenty-four. *Asian doesn't raisin*, a Hmong rec-league ballplayer once told me after he revealed he was forty-five. He looked half that.

She has the look of someone who's seen a lot in life, she's so even-handed. Whatever stereotypes I have of Japanese women, I'm expecting a high-pitched voice, very *hee-hee*, hiding behind her hands. But actually she speaks in a straightforward, Midwestern mid-register.

"Ricky, you look surprised to see me."

"To be honest, Vi—Principal Koda, I was expecting to find Principal McWhorter in here." My mind races. What if she was let go because someone narced on her for harboring me, a documented American dissenter?

"Oh, Principal McWhorter is doing fine. She's at home taking maternity leave. I'm filling in while she changes diapers and is able to devote herself to her child."

"Oh, thank God," I say, slightly slump forward.

"Excuse me?"

"Can I ask you a question, because we don't know each other that well."

"By all means."

"Is there anything different from Principal McWhorter that you expect of me?"

"I have high hopes," Koda says, makes a swiping motion with the flat of her hand to whump off dust on her desktop.

"High hopes?"

"High hopes."

"Principal, all due respect, I'm a janitor."

"No, you're a steward. It's a very important job, Mr. Powell. This is an ecosystem, and we all exist together. You matter. The things around us matter. They all have an energy. Whiteboards. Floors. Computers. You communicate with that energy." Koda brings her hands together to prove her point. "Your job is very important."

I feel like if this was random yammer from a street preacher, I'd dismiss him with a dollar bill or a shrug of indifference, but her maintaining steady eye contact the entire time makes me a true believer. I'd follow this woman to the ends of the earth.

"Yes, Principal Koda," I say, already obedient.

"Yes to what?" Koda asks.

"I am a steward."

"You are a steward."

"I am a steward."

CHAPTER THIRTY-FIVE

I DIG THE grunt work. I'm getting used to my body again. Since it's my second rodeo at the high school, I'm familiar with the duties and demands: they're physical, but not entirely draining. I'm trying to feel comfortable in my own skin, but I still have times where I flash between old me, more recent me, and me now. I'm not the unbridled stallion of yore; I almost broke my fucking neck. And I had to relearn everything for a few months: how to piss, sleep, stand. But I'm not that guy, either. And I'm also not that strong-bodied me. I don't know who I am now, but I'm trying to figure it out step-by-step, task after task. What aches, what works. I'm a goddamned fawn doing that stupid dance, figuring out how to get its ass off the ground on four shaky legs.

Also, I have a new coworker, Yoel. He's younger than me, says he used to go to this high school three years ago. Yoel needs the money, but he's also working the Internet fame angle. Always sending Snaps or taking selfies of himself pouting in the bathroom. Pushes the working-man persona. The young babes must dig the blue-collar, cultivated look. Johnny Lunch Pail. But he also drives a BMW. And wears a cologne that he tells me is ninety dollars a bottle. Flexes that he has close to thirty thousand followers, because he made up a funny dance two years ago. Get your money, man—I have no ill will, but I wish he'd do a better job sweeping and mopping. I almost have to pull double duty when we're both working. I'm pushing bristles while this idiot finds the right golden-hour lighting to cast the shadows on his cheekbones.

One time I walk in on Yoel and he's wiping away mascara and what appears to be that powder that women lather on their cheeks to give them a good glow. Rouge? Anyway, he's wiping it away, and I walk into the shared bathroom area and he's startled and knocks a bunch of scrubs and creams and things into the sink.

"No, no," he says. "Fuck. Knock next time, Ricky."

"What's wrong, Yoel?"

"This shit is so expensive."

"Sorry, brother, go snag some from your mom."

"I pay for all of this with my own money."

"Are you making way more than me?"

"No, honey, not from this job. I'm a 'content creator,'" he says. "But it's still expensive."

Yoel tells me about how he fronts this macho posturing on his main IG, but on his finsta and other alts, he's trying to make it as a MUA or makeup artist. Only he pronounces MUA like when you're exaggerating a kiss. His father would never approve.

"I'm sorry, Yoel," I say. "Go buy yourself something nice." I slip him two fivers.

"This is like one-fifth of a palette," he says, but smiles.

CHAPTER THIRTY-SIX

I KNOW I'LL catch the Intertribal Council eventually, but I don't go out of my way to seek them out. Pilgrim is long gone. Grey Cloud is in charge now, with Tara as VP, and he's never been my biggest fan. Also, there's that whole thing about me being white. Do I write a note? Never bring it up? Drop the truth bomb and deal with the aftermath?

I don't have much time to chew on it, because I find out the rooms for extracurricular clubs have all been reassigned, so as I'm walking into a room to clean, expecting to find a bunch of D&D geeks locked into their swords-and-sorcery shit, I find the Intertribal Council huddled around a table.

"Ricky!" Tara says, gives me a wave. Her hair is still a dirty blonde but with a fringe of purple at the bottom. She's wearing circle-framed glasses, has at least three new piercings. Rocks the chic-nerd shit well.

A few of the other students nod or wave, give subtle smiles. A couple of newbies don't know me from a can of paint. Eileen stays silent, but her eyes read warmth. Grey Cloud looks at me and then brings his eyes back to the task at hand. The rest of them follow suit.

They're discussing an upcoming protest at the homecoming rally, is what I catch. Talking signs, chants. Tara mentions borrowing a megaphone. They seem really intent, faces serious. I change the liners and am out before I intrude. A container of chocolate milk was crushed inside the can, outside of the lining, but I'll double back later, get to it after the council leaves.

I'm in the gym cleaning up after Easy Breathing 101. Yoel told me it's a stress relief class. They lie down on the heavy mats in the dark while the PE teacher plays sounds of whales breaching or breathing. Kids can no longer fling dodgeballs or roll around on those knuckle-crunching "scooters." One class legit had a session called Funsketball, where they played basketball, but anything that even glanced the rim or the backboard counted. It's an easy knock to see this next gen as soft, but who wouldn't want to take a nap class? Frankie once called me a child for taking regular naps, but she laughed when I countered: "So, someone full of wonder and verve?"

I'm rolling up mats, when I get a kink in my neck. I don't want to push it, so I let the one I was rolling spring back flat and I take a quick break on top of it. Lie down and try to keep my back as straight as possible. Turn my head slowly to the right and left. I close my eyes, because I can focus better with the world dimmed. I can still hear the squeak of wheels from a basketball rack being rolled across the court, the bark of the gym coach trying to coax extra effort out of the students, the phys-ed-exempt gossiping on the bleachers. I don't know how much time has passed, but I feel a presence next to me. Someone else lying a few inches away, also controlling their breathing. Before I can ease back into a sitting position and see who it is, I hear her voice.

"They radiate energy outward," Koda says. "Thank them for their service."

"Out loud?"

"Out loud or in your own head. Whatever feels comfortable to you."

No lie, this is the most intimate interaction I've had in months. Nothing untoward, more like when an older sibling puts their hands next to yours to show you how to choke up on a baseball bat. Or when your aunt scratches your arm and you want to sit in that soothingness forever. I get the spine-tingling feels. I almost call her "Mom."

"Principal Koda—"

But then I realize that she's breathing deeply like she's nearing the end of something, and before I can get another word out, she's up and walking off, a clack of heels across the floor.

CHAPTER THIRTY-SEVEN

I GET INTO a routine. Work, go home, run. Lift weights. Yoga with Mom. I read self-help books with titles like *Living Your Best You* and *The Power of Me*. Go to bed at an early hour. Do the exact same thing six days a week. On Saturdays, I only do a light jog and hit other easy cardio. Sometimes I'll fill old gallon milk jugs with water and use them as free weights.

This goes on for a month. Two months. Three.

Soon, that belly I slapped is no longer present. Because it somehow seems appropriate, I also decide to cut off all my hair. Bye-bye, long locks. Buzz it clean, but leave the beard. Seems like the right time. Stare at my reflection in the mirror. Give myself a pep talk. Smack my face around a little bit. Take the shears to my head while "Whole Lotta Love" by Zepp blasts in the background.

Never again will I take my body for granted. Luckily, I'm young enough to bounce back. Comes a time we all break down. Age. Injury. Thank whatever higher power for the fact that I'm back to old, move-with-ease, strong-bodied me. No major aches and pains. These days won't last forever. I'll try my best to keep it up, be one of those obscene sixty-year-olds with a six-pack doing dips on a jungle gym. Or maybe not. Maybe the end of the road happens soon when I twist an ankle and go back to bad habits. Either way, I'll be easier on myself.

I exhale loudly through my mouth, inhale through my nose for four seconds, hold my breath for seven seconds, and then exhale for eight seconds. *I am a tender man, I am a tender man, I am a tender man.*

I'm close to my wrestling weight. I'll still hit the tanning booth on occasion, but only because vitamin D is scarce come the colder seasons, and also otherwise I'd be egg pale. I don't go dark; I only go for a healthy glow. Part of me almost requests the heavier tone out of habit, but I know better. Although I do miss how it made my abs look. There's a reason bodybuilders grease down. But although I'm in better shape, I'm not quite at performance weight anyways, so what would I be highlighting? Less six-pack than keg. No more hair dye, though. Only sporting my original blond locks.

I will say, my clothes fit better. I won't wear sweatpants ever again. I go to a Kohl's, because Mom has coupons. Try on jeans, shirts, new shoes. I'm trying to purchase my own clothes like an adult, but Mom insists on buying.

"Back to school!" she says, pulls the card out of the chip reader.

"Oh, how long have you been in college?" the cashier asks.

"It's for high school," I say, without thinking.

She must think I'm a genetic freak or a dummy who got held back. And although I do have a baby face, the beard helps age me.

Come to think of it, I have seen some students walking around with a good amount of facial hair. Not like mine, though. My beard is getting Viking-thick. I swear when I was in high school all the kids were rail-thin and acne-ridden. Kids today feast on hormone-pumped beef and GMO chicken drumsticks and get grown. So I go with it.

"High school?" she asks, waiting for confirmation.

"Yes," I say. "Here to buy my big-boy pants."

CHAPTER THIRTY-EIGHT

I CATCH GREY Cloud in the halls. Not sure if I should go for play-it-cool barely acknowledging him, or an earnest hey. I'm overthinking it when Grey Cloud gets within five feet of me.

"What's up, mayo?" Grey Cloud says when he sees me.

"You can't talk to me that way," I say, not sure if he's joking.

"You're not faculty, bro," he says, keeps walking.

"Nice hat," I say.

He stops. Turns. "Thanks."

"I meant that as a joke." For some reason my voice trips weird and makes it sound like a question. Doesn't push confidence.

"No shit," Grey Cloud says.

Next time I see him in the boys' bathroom, I say, "What's up, Grey Cloud?"

And he says, "What's up, White Broom?" He smells like smoke, but even if he's lighting up, I won't call him on it.

"Hey, can I bum one?"

"One what?"

"A cigarette, man. I'm no narc."

"Cigarette? What is this, the seventies?" Grey Cloud asks, pulls out his Juul, takes a huge hit, blows it into the air. I lean back and accidentally trigger the hand dryer. We sit in the whoosh.

I'm going to get this kid to like me if it's the last thing I do. No, I'm going to make this motherfucker love me. Feel like it's what Pilgrim would've wanted. Or at least for us to be on decent terms.

The next day, I see Grey Cloud sitting on the steps by himself outside of school. Looks like he's waiting for a ride. I walk past him, do that thing where I give a half head nod. If he acknowledges it, it's all good, but if he blows me off I can play it off as a crick of the neck. A sudden appreciation of the view.

I walk to my car, pull out my keys, try to juggle my Nalgene and backpack. I look back at Grey Cloud. He reads stressed. Keeps checking his phone, and he's not a constant phone checker as far as I've seen.

So I do what any adult would do in my situation. I drive off.

Actually, I drive up to him. Park parallel to the curb. Turn the engine off and gesture to him. He slowly rises, walks over. He's close enough that we can speak in hushed tones and still make out what the other is saying. His phone is tilted at me, and it looks like a ton of words typed out into his Notes app. Like he's workshopping a screenplay.

"English class?" I ask.

"No," he says, realizes what I'm looking at, turns his phone to him, swipes off the app. "Grocery list."

I've got to stop being coy with this kid. "Why do you hate me, man?"

"I don't hate you, I love you," he says, brings his line of sight down to the passenger seat. Reveals a dimple.

"What?"

"I'm fucking with you, man. I caught you for a second, though, right?" He looks like he's going to crack a laugh.

"You look stressed," I say.

"Planning shit."

"Homecoming? Did you ask anyone?"

"Nah, probably won't."

I'm no good at this. Finding the right words. Saying the things the older person is supposed to say. *Aim high. Believe in yourself. Fight for your right to party.* I would've never asked a girl to homecoming when I was in high school. You don't dare bend or break social norms unless you want to be an outcast. One year a kid sneezed funny and he had to transfer districts.

"Yeah, probably better that way," I say to fill the void.

"'Better that way'? Aren't you supposed to give me advice or something? You suck at this," Grey Cloud says, lifts his backpack, which was at his side, and slides a strap over each arm like he's getting ready to leave, but I don't see any ride within sight.

"I never had a dad."

"Shit."

"I'm over it. You should go with friends. The ITC kids."

"We'll all be there."

I feel like this is my shot. I've broken through a bit. I'm not getting completely stonewalled. "You talk to Pilgrim anymore?"

"Every once in a while."

"Is he coming to homecoming?" I mess with my rearview mirror even though the car is parked.

"Nah, man. Pilgrim is overseas doing his hoo-rah duty," he says, relaxes a bit. Leans against a railing.

"I never got the vibe he was particularly patriotic."

"Fuck no. He wanted to get out of Omaha. See the world on government money."

"Couldn't he have become a flight attendant?"

"You want Pilgrim's husky ass hovering over you asking you if you want a hot towel? I could barely sit next to the dude in the van on road trips. Fucking overactive sweat glands."

"Well, next time you talk to him, tell him I said, 'What's up?'"

"That's all you want me to say? 'What's up'?" He taps at his phone and pretends to exaggeratedly type in a few letters. Mouths, *What's up?* "Anything else?"

"Tell him I've been trying to get ahold of him. Tell him to look me up."

He mouths each word, types it into his phone. "Got it," he says.

"Let me see," I say. He turns the phone toward me, and I only see the words *FUCK OFF* typed over and over again. This dick. But he laughs for real this time, and I know we're getting somewhere.

CHAPTER THIRTY-NINE

MOM LINKS ME to this Facebook announcement. Tryout for a new wrestling promo, Total Hotshot Wrestling. Omaha's only got about a million people, maybe a little over with all the adjoining areas. Like many midsize American cities, we have too much of what we don't need and not enough of what's necessary. Glut of wrestling promos, but almost no vegan restaurants. I could point a hose in the air and the comedown would douse a singer-songwriter. And yet we lack in paved skate parks.

Three wrestling promotions are now prominent in town. Pro Mag, WOW (World of Wrestling), and Total Hotshot Wrestling. THW is the newest comer and looks to be kicking up dust by antagonizing Pro Mag, which is the biggest player.

Total Hotshot has a small roster, but their champion "attacked" the Pro Mag champ, Billy Joe Babcock, outside of the Waiting Room, and ran away with the Pro Mag belt. This resulted in Billy Joe shooting a promo that was released on YouTube and Facebook, where he kept referring to it as "Total Hot-Shit Wrestling."

I'm game for anything that runs against Pro Mag. My doc had said to take it easy on any serious physical activities, especially ones that could potentially put my neck in a bind. But would you tell a dragon not to spread its wings?

After I get off my shifts, I change out of my janitor threads and throw on old basketball shorts and sneakers and head to the track. Benson has a quality track, and it's off-season, so it isn't in heavy use. Except the girls' soccer team practices on the football field, which sits inside the track. To avoid any gossip about me as a weirdo gawker, I run with my head down and keep my eyes on the track right in front of my feet. Look like I'm trying to find a lost contact lens that just keeps rolling out of reach.

Doing the eyes-on-the-prize shuffle, I accidentally run into Heyleigh, a dewy youth on the dance squad. Her sharp facial features remind me of an actress playing Joan of Arc, and she's wearing a face full of makeup while running in a sheer tank top and short shorts. Her blonde hair is pulled into a ponytail.

"Hey, killer."

"I'll kill you," I say, not thinking it through.

"Ugh, please murder me," she says, winks, runs away.

I don't get their slang. You can't joke about minor violence, but these kids routinely crack lines that make me blush. Feels like there's always been this socialized wiring of getting hot at the thought of murderers from Jack the Ripper days to true-crime podcasts. Or even casting that chisel-jawed young doofus as Ted Bundy. Whatever happened to the straightforward nature of saying what's in your heart? I wear my emotions like a too-big band patch on the sleeve of my jean jacket: stupid obvious.

She's super cute, but obviously that's a gross no-no. When Heyleigh laps me her second time around, she gives me the peace sign and then drops her pointer finger to flip me the bird. Then she sticks her tongue out and takes off again.

"Come back," I whisper, when she's already too far ahead. Indecent, but I do get a little burst in knowing I've still got it.

Eventually, I stop jogging and trot to my car like I realized I left my electric kettle on at home.

CHAPTER FORTY

EARLY MORNING, AND it's so wild bright we have to shield our eyes. Fifteen of us mill around outside of this boxing gym–slash–cardio kickboxing facility. Most of us are holding cups of coffee. One guy is doing sprints to keep his blood flowing.

I don't need that flash. That's rookie shit. For me it's more mental. I did all the physical prep. Drank coffee. Took a shit. Ate breakfast. Took another shit. Did some stretching. Got loose. Drove over here. *I've been here before*, I keep telling myself. *I've been here before. Easy as riding a bike.*

I need this; I feel like if any of this is meant to work out, this is my final hurrah. I only have a few years left where the mat and the splashes won't wreck my body. And the neck injury definitely kick-started the wear and tear.

I feel an unexpected pang of nerves in my stomach. It's been a long time. Do I need to take another shit? I have to wrestle with my neck in mind, but not be so conscious of it that I'm pulling back and selling it soft.

A giant man with a chest as wide as a mattress comes out to unlock the door. He's wearing a green tracksuit, and he smells like cheap cologne. Too alcoholic, but with a slightly sporty scent to mask it. Burns the nostrils if you get too close.

We all funnel into the brightly lit gym. I lag back. Last one in. Mats are lined up on the side. Heavy bags and speed bags hold steady. Racks and racks of free weights. Battle ropes that sit thick on the floor. Stacks of boxes for people to practice jumps on are lined up against the wall.

A cardio class is off to the side doing their stretches while a young woman with a high ponytail is already sweating and yelling motivational sayings at them. The class is almost all women.

The ring is set up off to the side of the cardio class. It looks haphazard. The ring ropes don't seem taut. A stain on the apron makes it look like someone took a giant piss in the middle. The room smells like armpits and feet.

Most of these guys are around my age. Some younger, a few older. Bodies of all shapes and sizes. Some lean. Others not. Some came dressed to impress. Hand-stitched or store-bought costumes slightly altered. A dragon. A plumber. A doctor. Others in gym clothes. Most aren't ready for this. I can tell because they look like kids lost in department stores. Wide-eyed and trying to catch every bit of info. Signing waivers, taking it all in. They're too new. If you've never wrestled before, your body isn't ready for it. Being an ex-athlete helps, but wrestling is its own thing. Thinking you'll be good just because you played football or even wrestled collegiately is wrongheaded. This is cardio and back bumps and knowing your body and the body of your partner. Being intimate with the ring as well.

Soon as I make my way into the room, lagging back after the crowd, I look into the eyes of the promoters, and they all look like they recognize me. Three guys sitting behind a folding table. One of them has muttonchops and an acne-scarred nose. The other two are skinny and dark-haired in that way that all skinny, dark-haired guys get mistaken for each other.

Chops points over in my direction, asks the dark hairs a question behind his hands. The others look me over again. Suddenly, I feel my back tighten up. Heat creeps up my neck.

I drop my duffel bag and jog in place, trying to keep the blood flowing, when the two dark hairs look at me and one asks, "Do I know you?"

"Nope," I say, still jogging.

"Sure, I know you."

"Face doesn't ring a bell."

"Aren't you Bobby Machete?"

I keep jogging, and in one swift motion, I scoop up my bag and keep moving my legs right out the front door to my Mustang. Pretty sure someone behind me laughs.

In my car, I blast AC and music (Maiden because I was listening to my old intro before walking in) and start punching the shit out of the roof. If they knew who I was, there's little chance that conversation veers into positive affirmations and back pats. All that hard work. Getting back to my regular weight. Working out even further to get into wrestling shape. Eating right. Getting to bed early. Staying focused. Hell, I even skipped jerking off the last three weeks. An old trainer's myth, but I was betting on the idea that the pent-up energy could do me good in the ring.

"Fuck! Fuck! Fuck!"

I keep screaming and punching the roof. Finally, hand hurting and exhausted, I look outside and see that I'm still sitting idle in the parking lot, a stranger with a brown backpack staring at me. A straggler coming in late and pausing to see my spectacle.

I put my car in drive. Drive.

I pull up at a DQ. Get me the biggest goddamn Blizzard with everything on it. Heap that thing with all the ice cream, syrups, and pulverized candy bits.

I sit in the parking lot at DQ and eat my Blizzard with my red spoon. I also snagged a box of cherry Dilly bars. I pull one out. It's melting. I take the thing down in three bites, red running down my wrist like I'm a nerd at high altitude with a bloody nose. Fuck.

I lose my cool. I slam my fist into my Blizzard. The ice cream actually eases the pain in my knuckles. I keep slamming it, making a mess. Chocolate and ice cream and crushed-up candy fly everywhere. Tears flow. But not tears of pain, tears of frustration.

A young Tom Hanks would've handled it much more levelheaded. Heard his name and probably whipped on Ray-Bans, done a spin, pointed at them, and then walked out, the King of Cool. Not a motherfucking wreck in this Dairy Queen parking lot, all snot and tears and ice cream hands. Ricky Versus the Blizzard.

CHAPTER FORTY-ONE

CAFETERIA CRIMES ARE basically low-grade. No one's trying to smuggle steam-table pans of pizzas. At worst, they lift an extra chocolate milk. Cut in line. Crib homework. Two reasons for the lack of riffraff: the cafeteria gets lit up like a church through natural lighting. Shine light and people show their best behavior. Second, their curriculum is no joke. No one has time to fuck around lest they only get accepted into their safety school.

It's midday in the cafeteria, and I'm monitoring the general upkeep. Emptying trash cans and cleaning up an orange juice spill. Suddenly, a minor flight of violence breaks out. Nothing serious. Two students griping over a girl. Or the existence of a girl who lives two districts over and the only evidence is a blurry IG photo. Less fisticuffs and more trays being jostled and food being sent aloft. But if high school students even sniff something resembling conflict, they'll circle and begin instigating.

High school in my day was brutal. Senior year, a girl threw another girl twice her size through the trophy case, almost killing her. Two weeks later, a student stabbed a pencil into the neck of a security guard. Once, a student passed out from a seizure in the bathroom and instead of helping him, his peers recorded it and posted it to Facebook. Never heard from him again.

But this, this seems trivial. The two dudes have their hands now on each other's shoulders, jockeying for position. No punches thrown. No pencil thrust into a soft spot.

I grab Dude One and separate him from Dude Two. Tell them to calm their shit.

"Greg, relax," I say.

"My name's not Greg," Greg says. They're both big boys, probably wrestlers or football jocks trying to flex macho in front of their peers. The pudding faces could literally be brothers. Same mop top. Same acne. Same little hairs playing facial hair pretend.

The air is electric in anticipation, and I can tell for a split second that Dude Two is considering giving me a run for my money. Wants to take a swing at me just to see what would happen. They're already in trouble; why not see where this goes?

Whenever you get around young kids, college-age especially, but even late high school, you forget that that's when everyone's at their physical peak. Hard bodies with idiot fizz. I lock my arms around both boys. Dude Two is putting up a little bit of a fight. Not trying to break free, but not exactly going willingly. He's strong. But I'm stronger. I'm a grown-ass man. He's still a growing boy. Probably goes home to his mom microwaving him Hot Pockets, which I'm not knocking. He knows it, too. He can feel me push against him with relative ease. Why can't he go easy like Greg?

Vice Principal Koda shows. Flanked by two security guards. She's wearing a gray power suit. Her eyebrow rises, and she points her thumb behind her, as in *Get your asses to my office*. Both boys quickly fall in line. Koda has that kind of power. Dude Two pauses to pick up his tray and a stray apple. An overturned chocolate Snack Pack. She nods at him, but I make a motion with my hand like, *I've got this.* He looks at Koda and bends back up, goes to her office with Greg. The two security guards follow. Koda gives me a thumbs-up, and it's easily the best one I've received this year.

CHAPTER FORTY-TWO

TWO DAYS AFTER my semipublic failure and private freak-out, I'm wiping down whiteboards when Grey Cloud walks into the Intertribal Council room. Pre-meeting, it's only the two of us and an audience of empty desks. He looks at me and I look at him and we both wait for the other person to start yapping. But this is different. No cuts, no jabs, no ribs. He looks at me like he needs to drop a coin and make a wish into a well. The analog clock ticks so loud I swear the minute hand is giving us the finger.

"What's the deal, Grey Cloud?" I ask. I'm standing at the board, holding a spray bottle of cleaner and a damp rag. I feel a little more comfortable being straightforward with him.

A few days before, I overheard one of the counselors talk to an instructor about radical empathy. Modeling honesty to let the kids know you're on the same page. Showing your empty hand to someone who might read you as a threat. I don't know. That might be wrong. I was dry-mopping in a different corner of the room when I caught the info. Regardless, I have to show my hand. I put down the cloth and bottle.

"I'm all right, man," he says, rustles around in his backpack.

"Can I tell you something, Grey Cloud?"

"That's something."

"For real."

He sits down, tips his ball cap up a touch, so that I can clearly see his eyes. I take a gulp, and it feels like my heartbeat is coming from outside of my body. I hear shoes scuffing floors in the hall. Friendly banter. A locker slam.

"I'm white," I say.

"No shit," he says like I told him the sky isn't always blue.

"Well, I'm not one hundred percent sure. I just found out. It's likely."

"You sound like you just got a bad prognosis. I've been knowing. This is your big reveal? That you're a Pretendian?"

"How'd you know?" Now I have to take a seat at an adjacent desk.

"C'mon, man. You think you're the first white guy who heard a whisper about a grandfather or uncle who had some Native blood, took that tall tale, and ran with it? We live in Nebraska. Every white person out here thinks they're one-sixteenth. Makes 'em feel better so they can justify buying their kids backyard tipis from Target."

"No, but, like, deadass, I didn't know. I thought I was half-Native. I recently found out that's probably not legit." I run my palms back and forth across the desk.

"I figured you didn't know. Because if you did, that'd be some crazy shit. Like that lady who swears she's Black and tried to pass off her adopted brother as her son. Only a sociopath would keep it up. But you copping to it is a start. Also, I know you and Pilgrim are good, and Pilgrim is my dude."

"How do you know you're Native?"

"I looked in a mirror," he says.

"No, I mean, remember when the news was all ablaze with that white-ass-looking governor holding his blood test to prove his identity?"

"Look, man, if you really want to know, I'll AirDrop you a couple of articles. The one thing I can tell you, although I don't know much about the 23andMe bullshit, is that being Native isn't about blood samples. You have to be recognized by a tribe. It's about culture. Community," he says, playing with his bag again. The nervous hands of wanting to be done. The shuffling together of shit before the bell has rung. But there's no bell.

"Thanks, man," I say, lean forward in my desk. The chair gives that might-slip shudder, but holds steady.

He pulls pieces of paper out of his bag. When they're slightly fanned, I can make out the names of the council with responsibilities listed underneath. Looks like Tara and he are doing most of the heavy lifting. Grey Cloud stacks them neatly. He takes his hat off, wipes his brow for a second, but he's not sweating, and the room is air-conditioned to a crisp seventy degrees.

"You good?"

"Anxious about this thing," he says. Fidgets with his hands. Plays with his gauges.

"Thing? You mean the protest."

"Yeah, the protest," he says, not trying to hide it. Knowing I know.

"Why?"

"There's ten, maybe twelve, of us on the best day. We've got allies in other groups, but even still, we're going to be outnumbered. And I want to make sure we're heard, but also that everyone is safe."

"Aren't these high school–sanctioned events usually safe?"

"Last year, I was part of another group protesting gun violence when a parent of a kid who doesn't even go here anymore caught wind of it and made threats on Facebook. Said something about how it'd be a shame if his truck jumped a curb and caught some kids."

"Jesus," I say, shake my head. A student runs by the classroom door singing a pop song off-key. Another girl follows who's wearing the same skirt.

"This other time a group proposing proper sex ed got a bomb threat called on their rally. Used to be Pilgrim leading these things, and even though he's one guy, he's a big guy. And we always felt a little safer behind him. But now that responsibility falls on me."

"Have you considered going to Principal Koda? She seems pretty on the level. She's Asian. Aren't y'all related?"

"Me and Koda?" he asks, gives me a quizzical look.

"No, I mean like Natives and Asians? Or is that racist?"

"Yes. Also, we can't go to Koda, man. Koda is a cop. She's too by the book. She'll never let us do it."

"Why not?"

"Dude, did you know one of the largest manufacturers of ICE detention centers is a Japanese woman who said her company was inspired by her family's background in internment camps?" he says. Shakes his head.

"So you don't like Japanese women?"

"No. That's not what I'm saying at all. I'm saying just because someone looks like they're on your side doesn't always mean they're on your side."

"So no Koda," I say, tapping the desk with my finger.

"No Koda."

"Okay, well, if you're worried about safety, I'll be there. I promise I'll try my hardest to keep y'all safe," I say, trying to be radical. Show my hand. Pick up my bottle and rag.

Later, I'm clocking out for the day when I realize I have a text message from Grey Cloud. He must've sent it right after I left the room. It's a link to a grainy YouTube video of protestors at a city council meeting. Not sure what they're arguing against, but the comments reveal that they're upset that a police officer got off scot-free after murdering an unarmed Black child. A young Black protestor shouts through a megaphone, and as police officers converge to arrest him with clearly angry intent behind their actions, a few fellow protestors, white and Asian, create a barrier between the cops and the Black man. And as if an invisible force field exists, the cops don't storm their fellow light-skins. The Asian woman even has dyed-blonde hair, as if that gives her extra deflection powers. You have to put your skin on the line. I've already got the blond locks.

CHAPTER FORTY-THREE

JOHNNY SENDS A random text. No words. A photo of Macho Man where he's dressed in a tie-dye undershirt and jeans. He's peering into the distance, sitting casually on a pier with his WWF Intercontinental Championship belt wedged underneath his ass.

I reply, *what do you want*
i'm sorry ricky
out of fucks to give

Tempted to send him back the gun emoji, but unfortunately, they nixed that shit and replaced it with a water pistol. And a plastic pistol with the safety tip doesn't send the same message.

But really, I don't even blame him. He's a looker but doesn't know a bad omen until it destroys his life. Once he told me that the real reason he left Germany was that his cousin got into heavy debt betting on greyhounds with gang-affiliated guys, but it was all a setup and it turned out the greyhounds were juiced on cocaine. They were shitting while they ran, which gave it away. Anyway, his cousin owed a few thousand and couldn't pay up, so Johnny went and got physical with the creditors before they could. Only they were better connected than Johnny imagined, so he had to skip town. Skip the country.

My phone rings. I pick up out of instinct and also because it almost frightens me. I can't remember the last time I actually talked on the phone. "Listen, I'm not coming back."

"That's not why I'm calling."

"So you don't want me to come back?"

"No, Marfa is here now."

"Why the text?"

"You owe me money. For the trip you never took."

"That was won fair and square."

"Ricky, you know it was a loan."

"You'll get your blood money." It's near Halloween. Brisk October weather. I imagine stuffing the money inside of a rotting pumpkin. I tell him as much.

"What's wrong with you?"

"You snaked my girl out from under me."

"She made the choice herself, Ricky."

"Hey, is Townes there?"

"Not right now, why?"

"Give him this message for me."

"What is it?"

I hang up on him. Then send him a GIF of Gallagher smashing a watermelon. *this is you*

that's a watermelon, not a pumpkin

not in America

Then the dots in response. Then they stop. Clearly something being deleted. Double-checking whether or not he actually knows what a pumpkin is. Which means I win.

CHAPTER FORTY-FOUR

YOEL TELLS ME Koda is looking for me. Wants a word. I try to get a vibe from him about what she wants, but he gives me the fuck-if-I-know shrug.

I finish buttoning up my jumpsuit then head toward her office.

I walk in and she's not there yet, so I take a seat. She's redecorated.

A few new photos: Koda graduating in her PhD robes. Weird that the more advanced you get, the more tricked out your sleeves. A photo of what I assume is her family. Her and her husband and two chubby-cheeked Japanese toddlers. They're all dressed like they're at a beach, but they're standing in front of Mount Rushmore. Her husband is a tall and regal-looking Japanese dude with a sharp jawline and a thin nose. He could be an actor in a movie where Scarlett Johansson stars opposite him as his Japanese girlfriend.

There's also a shrine of sorts and at the center is what looks like a large metal acorn attached to a thick, red-braided cord. I look outside the glass window and see the office folk doing their office work: answering phones and typing important emails.

I can't help it. I pick up the acorn and realize it's lighter than I expected. I also thought there would be a deep, gong-like sound, but it rattles around like a child banging pots and pans. I look outside and notice them not noticing me, so I pick up the acorn and spin it around and around and it makes a racket.

"Please put that down," Koda says, standing behind me for who knows how long.

"I'm sorry," I say, and put down the giant nut.

Koda walks in and shuts the door behind her. Usually, there's an open-door policy unless some serious shit is about to transpire. She doesn't close the blinds, so I know she won't slit my throat and dispose of the body, but I'm still worried about what she's going to say.

"Ricky, we have some big responsibilities."

"Big responsibilities." I read somewhere that the trick to getting people to like you is to mimic their actions and words.

"You and I have some of the same responsibilities, Ricky."

"The well-being of our students," I say. Lean back a little bit. Give the allure of confidence.

"Do you know why we can search their lockers?"

"Because we're the feds?"

"It's because we're their legal guardians while they're under our watch. I hear rumors about a protest at the homecoming pep rally," Koda says, leans forward. She really enunciates "pep rally." "I only want to avoid anyone getting injured. You want the same, right?"

"I'm no snitch, Principal Koda." My hands are sweating, and I'm definitely giving it away, because I keep rubbing them along the wood armrests.

"I can't put a stop to it beforehand, but I have some guesses." She pauses. "Ricky, do you know why major corporations disallow their employees from discussing wages? It's the same mentality. Coax them with talk of family and silence. But the ones at the top will always play the others as pawns. Silence is giving them power."

She's Jedi-mind-tricking me, and I'm on the verge of breaking.

"Please help me, Ricky."

"Can I get some water?"

"Didn't I see you at the water fountain filling up a Nalgene?"

"I have to get sixty-four ounces a day."

I stand and Koda stands a split second after like she thinks I'm going to run for it, but we both know that'd be absurd.

I suddenly realize maybe she's mirroring me.

I need to make a move, get out of here unscathed, but also avoid any more prodding. I'm not good under this type of duress.

Koda approaches and makes eye contact, but almost like she's looking through me. She actually puts her hand on my shoulder. "Ricky, we have a good working relationship. Please. Trust me. We both want what's best for the students, right? What's best for the school? For all of us."

Not sure what takes over me. I've been watching too many early nineties rom-coms starring Tom Hanks. I go in for the kiss. I'm not expecting any real sparks between us, more I just need to break the tension. I'm no goon. I'm not forcing myself on Principal Koda. I just pucker up and slowly move in, almost turning my head as I do it, recoiling even though I'm the one initiating the action. I feel like if I could see myself from her angle, I'd look like I was almost crying, my face screwed up. Dumb fucking move as far as dumb fucking moves go, but at this instant I need an out and I need her to give it to me. Before I crack and reveal all.

Koda puts her hand to my lips. As in *stop*. "Please get your things and get off the premises, Mr. Powell. I'm disappointed in you." She leaves me with the single worst words she could've said.

Yoel walks me to our lockers. "Principal Koda told me to escort you out," he says. "What happened back there, Ricky?"

"I did a stupid thing," I say. I throw a bunch of my personal effects into my Jansport. I hand my broom to Yoel. "This is yours now. Don't cry when I leave."

"You know I just have to put this back, right? The broom closet is literally behind you."

"Shhh," I say, put my finger to his lips to get him to stop talking. I can feel the moisture from his lip gloss.

CHAPTER FORTY-FIVE

NEED A NEW job, get on my feet. Nothing's biting. I borrow a little money from Mom. Promise to pay her back with interest.

When I fill out job applications, I have to scribble in and cross the right boxes.

Name, address, education, occupation.

Race.

Race.

Race.

White.

Like Miley Cyrus.

Like the Pope's clothes.

Chalk.

Milk.

Polar bears.

Whitewash.

White lie.

White knight.

White noise.

White chocolate.

Ghosts.

Europe.

TED Talks.

What does it mean to be white? Nothing. Zero. Packing peanuts. Styrofoam. Barely more than air. A fart. I guess I have to figure it out.

I sign my name over and over.

CHAPTER FORTY-SIX

MOM GENTLY WAKES me from one of those too-late-to-do-you-any-good, rise-from-the-dead naps. Spit dried on the chin, hair mashed into a right angle. Night now, but my internal clock is all screwy. Feels like dawn is breaking right as the sun goes down. Mom tells me to get showered and that we have to be somewhere. She nods at a few T-shirts she's set out, which is a weird juke considering she hasn't pulled that level of motherly doting since I was in elementary school, but maybe me sleeping in my old bed has brought back those old feels.

"No work today?" she asks, pats me on the forehead before I jump in the shower. I haven't told her I was fired. Does she know? I consider while I scrub up. God, I can never keep anything from Mom. She's like Instagram targeted ads; you only ever even whisper the word "Crockpot," and suddenly it's Crockpot after Crockpot clogging up your feed.

For the past week, when I should've been at work, I've been going to Blue Line in Dundee, ordering a cold brew and a plain bagel with sun-dried tomato spread, and using their free Internet to browse for work. The barista I was in love with has quit. Replaced by a skinny kid named Lance who's mean.

I've considered selling sperm, donating blood, using all my bodily tactics.

Dundee paints itself as ultra progressive, but really it's a bunch of white yuppies. Dundee is where all the old millionaires used to live. Brick facade homes. Crawling vine. Warren Buffett's billionaire ass. I thought about stalking him and begging for a handout.

Mom and I get in my car and she tells me to head downtown. Even though it's no more than a fifteen- to twenty-minute drive from her house, I haven't been downtown in years. It's tourist and art nerd central, with their lofts and communes and cobblestone paths. Restaurants where you can drink wine street-side and eat fresh-baked bread and preserved meats and other fancy-pants-type eats.

We pull up to the CHI Health Center, which used to be the Century-Link Center and before that was the Qwest Center. It will no doubt be bought out by another major corporation in a few years. I just hope it's something good, like the KFC Yum! Center or Smoothie King Center or Talking Stick Resort Arena. Give us a better sponsor than health care.

The CHI Health Center is a giant arena for Omaha: glass-enclosed skywalks, giant banquet halls, at least twenty thousand seats. A brass art display out front of kids doing jazz. I hate coming here. It's a whole ordeal. Finding parking. Walking. So many people in their dungarees. I've been here maybe five times in my entire life. And two of them were graduations. Not a fan of the pageantry. But as we walk toward the center, I immediately notice my folks: painted faces; T-shirts with muscle bound men posing in their underwear; large-script, scrawled-on signs. Wrestling fans.

"WWE?" I ask Mom. The WWE used to travel to Omaha all the time way back when, but as the organization got bigger, our burg got to be less of a need-to-hit hot spot. They circle around every few years.

She hands me the tickets like I'm a child who wants to have the ticket taker rip them at my first flick. Good seats. Real close.

I hold them up as if asking a question. "I could afford them," Mom says. Then I realize there's a third. Riley, Mom's new beau. This will be our first face-to-face. Not sure if this trip is about me or about meeting him.

Riley is slow-creep handsome. Not like a lethargic pedophile; what I mean is he's the kind of handsome you don't recognize at first. Comes to you in stages. You realize it after a while, even though it's been staring you in the face. He has kind eyes and smells like firewood. But not deep-woods firewood. Like suburban dad with a spiderwebbed stack next to the shed.

He gives me a firm handshake when we meet.

"Don't pee on me, okay?" I mutter under my breath.

"I'm sorry?" he asks.

"I said, 'Nice to meet you, Riley,'" I say, trying to salvage it.

We both do that thing of not meeting each other's eyes beyond the first blush and both look to Mom to bridge the gap. Riley's also holding a folded poster board.

"I didn't have time to write on it," he says, sheepish, and pulls out a thick black Sharpie.

We find our seats after waiting, and it's the first time in a long time that I get anxious. Excited. I haven't been to a wrestling match in months. Also, these are the pros. The lineup is stacked, strong from top to bottom. The Miz. Daniel Bryan. AJ Styles. The New Day. Charlotte Flair. Becky Lynch.

"Ricky, go get us some sweets, will you? Sodas, too," Mom says, hands me a few folded bills. "On me."

When I return, I see Mom holding a sign that says GO RICKY! I almost burst into tears on the spot. Feel that back-of-the-throat tickle of real emotion. Mom. Always being a mom.

"Can I hold it?" I ask.

"No, this is mine," she says. She waves it proudly. Riley even takes a turn.

When we get home, Riley bids us good-bye and drives off. Mom and I watch him recede, and then we go inside and rehash all the exciting shit we witnessed. My favorite match was Becky Lynch vs. Charlotte Flair. The Man vs. The Queen.

We drink beer bottles on the front porch swing. Late night, but the moon is showing off; it's a full-circle pink glow. Super Mega Werewolf Moon or whatever dumb name those space cadets hand down. I get it. It's all marketing. They keep giving these hues and shades names, and we keep tweeting about this sky rock. It's too cold for mosquitoes, but crickets somehow play their song. I swear it smells like suntan lotion, but my mind is playing tricks on my nose.

"Riley was nice," I say.

"Nice? Oh, he's more than nice."

"I'm going to ignore that. What I mean is that he seems like a genuine guy."

"You mean he didn't whip his dick out and spray you with it?" Mom almost can't get it out without laughing.

"Well, the CHI Health only has individual urinals, so we'll see what the future holds."

We clink our beers. Mom downs hers, pulls a fresh one, pops the cap into the grass.

"The sign. Real class act," I say.

"My idea, but he got on board and found all the materials. He's a sweetheart."

"That's good, Mom. You need more of that."

"What about you?"

We sit in the heaviness of that question. A dog whimpers one house down.

"You should go."

"Like to bed? The days of you being able to yap those commands are long gone, lady."

"You know what I mean. I can see it in your face." Mom stares at me, but I look away. Keep my eyes on the lights of the faraway antenna towers. Not sure if a dim star or a distant plane flickers in and out.

"Yeah, you're right. I should. I should see him."

"The moon looks beautiful tonight."

"Oh, the Stupid Werewolf."

CHAPTER FORTY-SEVEN

DAD, FATHER, POPS. Roy. Mr. Templeton. Not sure what to call him. What I do know is that he lives in Green Bank, West Virginia, which is apparently as off the radar as you can get. Thing about being that off radar is, it gets you next to a big-ass telescope. The country's largest. Close to five hundred feet tall. Dish so wide it can hold a Huskers game inside. This huge white framed behemoth that looks like a movie prop. Some site for two superheroes to duke it out at the world's end. It's located in the National Radio Quiet Zone, and so, to be allowed to live in their digs, you have to agree to no microwaves, no cell phones, no Wi-Fi, no nothing that emits radio waves. Messes with the scope. Also, it's in a pocket of the Alleghenies called Pocahontas County.

I drive up to Green Bank on WV 92 S and immediately notice its beauty. It's nestled inside the Allegheny mountain range and has a familiar feel minus the hills and mountains. Trees claustrophobically line the streets, and people are out conversing, shaking hands. A throwback to olden times in Any City, USA.

I pass by a group of elementary school kids during a soccer scrimmage. Parents sit in lawn chairs rooting on their kids for a practice that doesn't matter. American flags wave from almost every other porch.

Little wooden storefronts displayed on one street. A farmer on a tractor chugs along a side road. Though Omaha is a decent-sized city, I'm not completely unfamiliar with these kinds of environs. Nebraska has plenty of similar small towns.

Driving up to the city, my Internet access and phone service cut out.

Jonah, the Wi-Fi police, is a beardo with a serious sense of responsibility. He's wearing glasses, a brown denim jacket, and a dad baseball cap. Even his voice has a high whine typical of a tattletale. I admire his dedication, but I run into him fifteen minutes into town and he gives me a quick rundown that ends up turning into a long rundown. Basically he's a radio tech that patrols for any signs of satellite interference. He makes me sign a slip of paper that says I'll follow the rules.

I have a hunch everyone knows everyone's business in town, so when I first pull in, I grab a cup of coffee at a gas station to do some recon. Ask the older attendant with droopy earlobes—Sam, according to Sam's name tag—whether he knows a Roy Templeton. Sam points me in the right direction as I use my customer service voice and really play up the nice-guy act.

I have to use a map. Like a paper representation of a geographical space, with latitude and longitude and the whole nine. A key. I'm like, *Ancient wayfarers used this shit?*

I drive up to an old-fashioned two-story house. All wood. Chimney. Wraparound porch. I expect to find someone on the front porch whittling a sea lion while drinking sweet tea.

I knock on the door. A note that's taped there has drifted off and settled into the space between the door and the screen. I pick it up and it reads: WENT FOR QUICK TRIM. BACK SHORTLY. I don't know if this is meant for a specific person or if this is how they communicate here.

The barbershop is nearby. From outside, I see a middle-aged, prematurely graying, white gentleman getting his hair cut by a barber who looks like a character from an old-timey cartoon with racist crows. The whole scene reeks of bygone times: the spinning barber's pole, the white capes, the dusters. The long jar with the blue barber fluid and all the combs soaking like something out of a sci-fi lab.

I watch him through the blur of a dirty window. Know it's him. He looks like me. Don't need the paternity test to prove he's the dude. I have to calm my nerves, so I go back to my car and take two quick hits from my pipe before coming back to the storefront.

When he exits, he's whistling and looking at the ground, a magazine under his arm and little slivers of gray hair around his collar. He's wearing a fleece-lined corduroy coat and a red flannel underneath. His clothes look a little ragged, worse for wear. Young dudes will dress dapper if they have a reason: being a business professional or trying to impress a partner. But I feel like once you're spoken for or have little reason to get spiffed up, you pick one outfit and just wear it until you die. Might toss in a bucket hat for color.

He's easing toward a car, a mid-nineties-model Buick, when I call his name.

"Excuse, me, sir, are you Roy Templeton?"

Soon as he stops, gives me a once-over, I know he knows something. The look he gives off is of him questioning the world. Like the air quality has changed.

"Who are you?"

"My mother—Lena Powell—was a good friend of yours years ago."

"Lena Powell? I haven't heard that name in almost thirty years. Is she okay?"

I don't have a plan. All that travel: sixteen hours of staying awake and following the signs and the time deciding to make the drive and all the years before that and I still don't know what to ask. This is not the guy I pictured on the other end of this conversation. He's a nondescript white guy, the character actor always cast as a banker or a piano tuner. His hair is cut high and tight. Stylish, except it's his style before it became in style. His hands are worn and brown and darker than his face. He has a bit of age on him, but he still looks his age. I'd guess, if similar to Mom, around midforties.

"Uhm, she's sick," I fib. Come up with it right then.

"How sick? Sick enough to warrant you seeking me out?"

"It's not looking good." I hate to lie to the guy, but if Mom could fabricate a lie my entire life, I could chuck her into one. Also, it helps stretch the convo. Truth is she's probably sitting at home watching *Grace and Frankie* on Netflix or having a couple of those wine pouches with a few friends. Or scooting around town on her new Honda Dream 305.

"So, what do you need from me?" He still seems skeptical. Can't tell if he can see through my bullshit. He takes a long look at my face.

"Just a talk. Some stories?"

"Is it that bad? She can't talk?"

"I only wish she could say more." I don't. She's probably laughing her ass off as we speak.

"Follow me," Roy says, nods at his navy-and-brown Buick Roadmaster Wagon. Looks solid enough to drive through a wall.

I follow him to a coffee shop with a back porch that looks out on a scenic slice of West Virginia. Green and red-rust trees jam-pack the hills. Bet it looks awesome come autumn. A tiny farmhouse dots the landscape, but beyond that, there are little signs of human life for miles behind the coffee shop. Trees, trees, and more trees. A deer nips at grass like it's never even heard of a bullet. We both order two coffees, black, and I get a scone.

We sit on whitewashed wooden benches on the back porch. Another person, a woman around my age with a septum piercing, sits fifteen feet away from us, scribbling in a notebook. In any other town in America, this shop would've housed a dozen students tapping out emails and essays on laptops or aspiring screenwriters testing out their dialogue.

"Be careful with your crumbs," Roy says. "People pitch their leftovers into the woods and a family of coons will sniff around for handouts."

"There's a place in Omaha where they do the same thing with old chicken bones."

"Omaha, huh? Is that where she settled down?"

"Yes, sir, going on twenty-plus years," I say, sip my coffee. Glance at Septum Ring.

"Who did you say your pa was?"

"Jeremiah Twohatchet."

"Jeremiah Twohatchet?" Roy takes a breath.

"Yes, sir."

"Wow. That's a name I haven't heard in years."

"Did you know him?"

"Pardon my language, but he was a real sonuvabitch," Roy says, snorts. Lets loose a laugh. "We both pined for Lena during our college years. Lena was real sweet on Jeremiah, but Jeremiah kind of treated her poor. Nothing physical, but seemed to only really care about his own way in the world. Lena was a smart woman, always wise, but sometimes you can't outbrain the heart. She'd go back to him and often right out of my bed. I felt like a fool, but I was so in love with your mom. I followed her around like she followed him around."

We both sip our coffees. The fawn is gone. Nothing now but flora.

"You can call me Roy," Roy says.

"Thanks, Roy."

"Listen, if you're only out for stories, I can do you one better. I've got some old photos back at home, if you'd like. I can riffle around and find them."

I don't want to push it, but I feel like I need a memento, and asking for a selfie would be too weird. "Sure, much appreciated."

"I've also got to get back to feed Sandy."

I follow him back on the short drive to his place. Pass more throwback homes straight out of an American history textbook. When we walk up, I pretend like I wasn't here an hour ago.

Inside is a bunch of dark wood and lamps. Tons of tiny, ornate lamps. I want to ask why he doesn't get bigger lamps so he can lamp less. The couches also have that deep leather sheen. Like you can smell them from a picture. A stuffed dog (not previously dead stuffed, child's-plaything stuffed), tags actually attached to its collar, sits at the ready at the foot of a big recliner.

Roy checks his mail, sets it aside. We both take a seat in the big leather chairs. Sink in.

"Why did you come here?" I ask.

"Pace is real nice. Also, I have terrible migraines and other problems from certain sensitivities." He waves his hand in a wide circle in the air as if to say, all that out there.

The little I know about electrosensitivity is from Google-based reading on Green Mountain. Apparently, these people have symptoms that they feel stem from electromagnetic radiation. Doctors dismiss it, but the electrosensitive have hightailed it to Green Mountain because the lack of microwaves gives them a break from their pain. Who knows if it's real or he's a head case? It takes every ounce of me not to utter, *Ever try wrapping a bicycle helmet in tinfoil?*

"Did you come up here right after college?" I ask.

"Oh, no, I had a whole career as an engineer in Bismarck. North Dakota. Then I started to have these really bad headaches. Body aches.

No doctor could give me a straight answer. One thought it might've been a tick bite."

"So what was it?"

"Never got an answer, but all I know is that the source was a specific type of emitted waves. And once I found out about this place, it seemed like the only option. I've been here for over a decade. I admit it might be believing in the bogeyman, but even if it's a placebo effect, I've felt so much better since I've been here."

"Cheers to that," I say, and then make a motion to cheers, but remember that we're not drinking anything; that was a half hour ago at the coffee shop, and we both stare at my empty hand cupped as if holding a big mug of nothing. My fingers crumple back to a resting position.

"Anyway, I'm talking too much. I'm sorry to hear about your mother."

"Yeah, she's real sick, real sick."

"What is it? If you mind me asking?"

"Cancer. Lung cancer," I come up with, remembering how Mom in her college years used to smoke cigs like it was her religion.

"Wow. I'm so sorry." We both sit there, not sure how many more times we have to say we're sorry. "Let me see if I can track down those photos." He stands and disappears up a flight of stairs. A heavy walker. Good thing he lives in his own home, because any downstairs neighbor would want to murder him. I hear creaks and things overhead. Sounds like a drawer opening.

Not sure how long he's gone, but I immediately stand as soon as he goes upstairs. I walk around the room like I'm searching for a secret formula in a bad spy flick, but I'm not sure what I'm doing. I inventory everything: thick history books, particularly favoring presidential biographies; handcrafted wooden schooners; an assortment of pipes. Like I'm looking for clues, but I'm not sure to what end. I pull out my phone and take pictures. To show Mom later, I rationalize.

I even start touching his stuff. Picking things up, running my hands over their surfaces, and then putting them back down. A lot of the objects are thin-slicked, have the residue of wood oil.

For some reason, he's lighter on his feet on the way down. So light, in fact, that I don't catch him catching me snap the last two shots. He's directly to my left, holding open an old photo album. One of those older ones where you had to apply the photo to a sticky surface underneath a plastic cover. Think they stopped making those decades ago. He stares at me.

"You don't look like Jeremiah."

I stare at a schooner. Try to rustle up a good white lie. Figure instead on giving up the goods. I turn to him. "All right, listen. So, I'm not Jeremiah Twohatchet's son."

"Who are you?"

"Listen, I—"

"And why are you here?"

I need to come up with an answer fast, but all those improv seshes aren't helping. I wish Enid were here with her thick-ass glasses, cheering me on. I'd drop a sharp response. But even my small pause ruins the mood. Roy knows something is up.

"You should go," Roy says.

"Wait, no, wait." I put my hands out for some reason. Universal sign for *stop*.

"You should go," he says again, setting down the photo album on an old oak table.

And before I can get another word in, the old-timer is on me. Much more spry than he looks. He's got me in a headlock. I'm no longer sweatpants me, but I'm not exactly prime-time, either. Not after that tryout debacle. Also, he caught me by surprise, and he's got it locked in tight.

"Who are you?" he screams. "Who are you and why are you here?"

I can't get a word out because his arm is putting pressure on my windpipe. I'm about to pass out.

"Sandy, sic him, boy!" he screams, looking in the direction of the stuffed dog.

Right before I black out, I grab him by the testicles and squeeze. He's wearing thick jeans, but I've got ahold of something about the size of a kumquat. He lets go, and when I catch my breath, I stand and square up with him, lock him up tight, so he can't wriggle free. I have my arms wrapped around his entire torso, his arms down at his sides. We're chest to chest. I'm on top of his feet for a second, and I picture myself a preteen girl standing on his shoes to practice slow dancing before the middle school social. This isn't quite that, but there is an intimacy in how close we are, and he looks at me with the passion of someone wanting to commit a sin.

"Let me go," he manages to spit out between clenched teeth. Flecks of spit land on my face.

"I'm not here to hurt you," I say. "I just want to talk."

"You got a funny way of talking."

"You started it!"

"You look like the type of person to pull something sneaky. Trying to rob me? Take whatever you need."

"My type? I'm your type!"

"I'm not into boys," he says, then starts screaming for help before I throw him to the ground. He rolls harder than I would've wanted. Narrowly misses tumbling through an open door to what I'm guessing is the basement.

I take a second, hack out a few breaths. I grab his stuffed dog and run out of the house, leaving the door slammed behind me. I toss Sandy into the passenger seat and scrabble to get my keys into the ignition. I fly out of Green Mountain so fast, I hope Jonah comes after me and we can have a *Fast and the Furious*–style car chase wending through the mountains. Only Jonah isn't really a cop so much as he's a Wi-Fi narc, so his jurisdiction ends the second I can get one bar. Fuck that guy and fuck this town and fuck their dish and fuck astronomy and fuck these hills and fuck my dad and any square inch of dirt he's ever set foot on.

Not sure why he pulled the headlock. We both know I'm not Jeremiah Twohatchet's son. Although, after that fiasco, I'll never be able to explain myself.

I'm not sure why I grabbed the dog. I figure he owes me.

CHAPTER FORTY-EIGHT

NO DAD TRUMPS a shitty one. Right? Wind can't disappoint. Nothing can't beat you black and blue. I have so many friends whose fathers abused them. Who were never there for them. Who bought into the macho bullshit of the strong and silent, buzz-cut type. Ric Flair's son died of a black-tar heroin overdose because Ric Flair was Ric Flair and not a dad.

I'm better off is what I keep telling myself.

"Good fucking riddance," I say like I'm in an after-school special, but my audience is the fake dog that's sitting across from me inside of a highway-adjacent burger place. Not the clown or crown, but a small-biz knockoff.

Maybe those guys who went on dates with stuffed animals were secretly on return trips from having it out with their estranged dads and those were the last things they snatched, because now I'm downing a spicy chicken sandwich and my company is this fake dog with a collar and I sort of understand.

I'm losing it while gnawing on mushy fries. Stare at my feet because I don't want to cry inside this fast-food restaurant. It smells like old oil, and there's barely anyone in here except for teenage kids being mean to another teenage kid. The beeps of machines as the soundtrack. I hear a splash and a yell, but mind my own business. I go to the restroom, wash my face, return to my half-chewed sandwich.

Minutes later, I hear the get-out-of-here hustle of kids on the lam. I turn from my sandwich and notice the picked-on one drenched from what I can only guess was a Coke.

"Thanks for your help," he says without looking up, his hair hanging wet with what I imagine is the stickiest hair shellack.

"Here, kid," I say. I hand him the stuffed animal.

"I'm thirteen."

"Right, right," I say. I feel around in my pocket for a chunk of a half-wrapped edible. I put it on the dog's back like it's a tiny cowpoke. Give a quick "Giddyup!" Get back to my meal.

CHAPTER FORTY-NINE

I WISH I could lie low, process whatever the fuck that was in West Virginia. But I don't have the time, because homecoming is only two days away. Technically, I can't go. But I did make a promise to Jacob.

The theme is Remember the Eighties. Nostalgia from *Stranger Things* and *It* hits all the pleasure centers for the older faculty and administrators, plus kids who only know the era through video clips or online quizzes can get a real sense of it. Or at least a sniff at a sense. Thank God it wasn't something as hack as Under the Stars.

The part of my brain that makes the adult decisions—paying bills, drinking water, getting adequate sleep—tells me not to be here. But I want to see what Jacob and the ITC have in store. I have an idea that it'll involve picketing and signs, but I didn't witness any blueprints. They didn't want to leave any evidence for the higher-ups to confiscate, so they shared most of their details in WhatsApp.

I know if anyone sees me I'll get kicked out immediately, maybe even shown the door in a forceful manner: handcuffs, lights, the back of a squad car. I shave my beard. Dress up. Decide to grab one of those knockoff costumes that the packaging labels as EIGHTIES ROBOT MAN. It's a little before my time, so I have to Google whoever this is. Looks like the Cardi B album cover. Google tells me it's Max Headroom. No clue who that is, but I only need a costume that'll allow me to hide my face. This one comes with giant sunglasses and a prosthetic mask.

I park a few blocks away from the school. Not so far that a kid looking out his window would be frightened by this blond-haired maniac with a shiny suit on. But close enough to blend in.

The parking lot is full of cars done up with slogans in green and white paint markers. Streamers from bumpers. Balloons, so many balloons. It's a little chilly, so most of the students have jackets on over their outfits.

Tables with sweets on them to fundraise for the cheer squad. Tables covered in pamphlets and condoms to promote safe sex. A dunk tank.

I don't even know what school we're facing, but I find out as soon as I step in, and immediately it makes sense. The Millard South Indians. Mascot is a big racist caricature. His skin isn't red, but it might as well be. He's got an oversized nose and a headdress on. His clothes are a bunch of feathers and leather. Inside is a high school student yipping his or her heart out for the team, but it looks real bad. To make matters worse students and parents from the opposing school are also wearing headdresses, have their faces painted, chop their arms in tomahawk chants. Reminds me of when I played to a similar crowd.

Then I see Jacob and Tara and crew. Some white and Black students who aren't part of the Intertribal Council flock with them. They create a barrier with their bodies between the rough crowd. Altogether it's about twenty kids holding signs that say things like OUR CULTURE ISN'T YOUR COSTUME or PEOPLE AREN'T MASCOTS. The ITC members are dressed in all black and wearing face paint. They're also doused in fake blood and holding a giant banner that reads, YOU KILLED US AND NOW YOU MOCK

US. Kids on the protest side are recording with their phones. Likely live broadcasting it. Parents and students of both the opposing school and our own look pissed. Middle-aged moms and dads and their similarly attired offspring really don't want to do the mental gymnastics of why the protestors are testifying. The ones from Benson don't want anyone to upset their Friday-Night Lights. Grown-ass men and women make fists and shout slurs at literal kids.

"This isn't the time and place!"

Or: "It's only a mascot. This is homecoming!"

Some of it leaps straight to hate.

"Fuck you, Indians!" Only they pronounce it "Injuns" like they picked up a slang book from the early 1800s. Probably the same text that Donnie read.

"Fucking snowflakes. Go back to the rez!"

Faculty and staff attempt to keep both sides at bay, but it's getting hectic. The parking lot security guard, Tom Seguar, has a megaphone and is yelling at people to stay put. The chanting grows louder from the protestors. People jostle. Someone spits in the face of a student. Another person throws a drink in an adult's face. It's approaching bedlam. It feels like any second now someone is going to get seriously hurt.

Per usual, the protestors aren't the ones being violent, but security is starting to circle them. I see one of the guards grab Jacob, push him. Another is holding Tara's arms behind her back. Eileen is trying to shield Tara. This isn't even a large crowd compared to, say, the audience at a professional sporting event, but it's terrifying to be the minority among a group of people hell-bent on herd behavior. And that thinking is clearly *Let's get rid of these kids and get back to our pigskin and bigotry.*

No one's throwing punches, but there is a lot of yelling and shoving. Seguar gets flattened, and I'm right next to him when he loses his megaphone. Someone needs to stop the madness.

A car in the parking lot backfires, and people hit the deck, thinking either that it'll plow forward into the crowd or that it's a gun going off.

I grab the megaphone and scream, "Listen up, you white devils!"

They don't really hear me; someone says, "What?"

I take off my mask, put my glasses back on, then hit the speak button.

"Did you call us 'white devils'?" some dad asks. The crowd nearest me is listening. The ones who had hit the deck rise, dust themselves off. On the outer edges people are in their own social bubbles. A sense of unrest still works its way through the mob. But at least they're paying attention. I have this one moment to sway them. This moment right here. Otherwise, it could get even more destructive. Like when a wild animal wants to snap but you get it to focus, stroke its underbelly.

"What I'm here to say is we've been doing this for far too long. Natives are the true fucking Americans. We've stomped into their homes and told them what to do. Thrown them into foreign spaces. Slayed their babies. And we can't even agree on whether or not mascots should be Indians? This should be an easy answer. A small atonement, if anything."

"Who are you? Judge Judy and executioner?" a man in a camo shirt asks.

"You there," I say, pointing at him, a gentleman who looks to be forty-odd years old and is wearing rusted dog tags on top of the camo. "Did you serve, sir?"

"Why, yes," he says, slightly scooping up the tags with the underside of his hand for the crowd to see.

"And how do you feel when people wear camo gear or dog tags as fashion?"

"It pisses me off," he says, spits a little. Someone yells out the name "Timberly!" I ignore it.

"Why?"

"Because they never walked in our shoes. Because they'll never know."

"They can't walk in your shoes," I say. "Exactly. They can't walk in
your shoes! They can't walk in your shoes!" I say it over and over trying to get them to follow me. But it comes off like I'm inciting a flash
mob for a Zappos ad.

Not sure how teachers do it. I'm trying to get them to bridge the
gap, but everyone looks at me dumbfounded. Some are repeating my
mantra, but it's clearly not clicking. The crowd is getting restless. You
ever try to reach someone, and the second they feel condescended to,
they shut down? That's the crowd now. They're beginning to break
from their trance.

Everyone's staring at me. Like the great WWE Hall of Famer Macho
Man Randy Savage once said while he was juggling coffee creamers
in one of his best-ever promos: "In my moment of glory, I'm living in
a nightmare." As everyone stands at attention, right at their breaking
point, I don't know what else to say. You figure you're going to crush this
epic speech on that kind of stage and then you sputter out. Usually, I'm
killer on the mic, but this moment is too big even for me. I've got 'em
caught in a temporary daze, like when you see something unexpected
and almost don't know how to register it. But they're going to snap to
any second and either boo me, arrest me, pelt me with shit, or break out
into wild applause. Before they turn, I go for one final ace. I put myself
into position as the security guards move toward me.

I grab the Millard South mascot, who's been beside me the entire
time. I maneuver him or her in front of me. I'm too strong for this child,
and I'm sure he or she has barely any visibility in this giant Indian head.
I use a couple of coolers as steps and walk on top of a table, pulling
the mascot with me. Kick a bunch of the condoms off, and they fly into
the crowd.

I whisper "Tuck your chin" to the mascot, and I hear a teenage
girl's voice say, "What?" I push her head underneath my legs and then
lift her into the air and I hope she heard me when we drop and in one

fluid motion, I piledrive her through the table, taking the brunt of the damage with the backs of my legs. The flimsy table goes flat, and I'm on the ground, with the mascot slowly rolling away. Hope she's not in pain. But I think she's fine, because after we land, our bodies still absorbing the shock, I hear her mutter, "Whoa!"

The students lose their cool. Sound as loud as a jet turbine or a plastic bag of potato chips ripped open close to your ear. Next-level decibels. Rap-battle-in-the-schoolyard-style. Fistfight haymaker. "Did you see that?" a redheaded boy keeps screaming while holding his phone. I have enough wherewithal to realize that I have about a half second to get out of here before the adults collapse in on me. One security guard is in my direct line between the parking lot and my car. I'm a hero to these kids now, even the ones rocking headdresses, and they will not let their hero perish. These aren't the passive kids of yesteryear. These are walkout-and-petition kids. They don't let the security guards touch me. I can feel their hands, their fingertips propel me forward. Make way. Some pat me on the back. Yell affirmations in my ear. I can't see how their parents and chaperones are reacting, because I'm overwhelmed by their joy-filled faces grabbing at me like I'm the latest hot-shit content creator. They shield me and keep pushing security away. Reminds me of the worship of my fans. For a second, I want to bask. Oh God, do I want to bask. But I don't have the time. One guard almost gets me, but he grabs a fistful of wig, and it's too close, so I kick it into high gear.

I'd love to say I got off scot-free. High-kicked it out of there with my sunglasses still on. In fact, things are moving so slo-mo that I daydream about Pilgrim being here with me. I'm piggyback-riding him into the distance, him forearm shivering anyone who gets in our way. I'm holding tight around his neck, and he's moving as easy as a kid hitching up his backpack to catch the bus. And we're laughing, laughing, laughing, like people only do in commercials: full-mouthed, worry-free.

But in reality, I don't make it more than five steps. I'm set to turn on the jet fuel when I get speared by a security guard into a small sedan. My glasses fly off. Pretty sure I have a minor concussion, as I black out temporarily and come to in the back of an ambulance with handcuffs on.

The news is confused by my costume, keep calling me Cardi B. They make quick mention of why the students were protesting in the first place. Jacob is featured, with the tag STUDENT PROTESTOR on the chyron.

"Would you call him your hero?" a reporter with a big microphone asks Jacob.

"No."

Jacob gets back to the issue at hand about Native media representation, but they cut him off. Tease a new ice cream parlor for dogs after the commercial break.

CHAPTER FIFTY

MY VIDEO GOES viral. Or what passes for viral in today's oversaturated age. Meaning at most my bagel guy will recognize me. Over a dozen versions are spread over the Internet. The definitive one is from a teen who goes to Benson and was right beside me during the debacle. Got the best angle. No magic formula for going viral exists. You can crunch algorithms and try to fake it to make it, but a truly singular video involves a weird alchemy. Double rainbow guy. Chocolate Rain. "Charlie Bit My Finger." My vid has social justice, a guy dressed as an eighties character, and a public scene.

School doesn't press charges, because they know security overreacted and went full Goldberg on my ass, slamming my head and body into a sedan, leaving a me-size dent. Rumors are the student mascot's parents are threatening the school, but don't press me with litigation. I think they considered it, but realize they can get more scratch off the school. Also, the student ended up fine. Even increased her follower count.

A local newscaster, Bryant Silvestre, shows up at Mom's house. Wants to get a follow-up. Silvestre is a puffy, red-faced weatherman-turned–sports anchor–turned–sideline reporter. Not sure how the hierarchy works at news stations, but it feels like he's going the wrong way. They interview me in Mom's living room. She's arranged the begonias just so. Her miniatures are positioned in the background. Mom, off camera, is so proud.

"I did what anyone in their right mind would do. Don't be on the wrong side of history on this. Remember those white people screaming at Black folks at sit-ins are still alive. Ditto the white people holding dogs nipping at their limbs. They're the racist grandpas and grandmas that we see on holidays. Be the future you you want you to be," I say, and then when Silvestre turns back to the camera to sign off, I give a wild-eyed look and stick my tongue out, make the devil horns with my hands, because old habits die hard. "Okay," Silvestre says. He signs off. He turns to me right after and says, "Thanks, that was great."

I watch it on the six o'clock newscast.

Then again at ten.

I get a text message right after the ten o'clock rerun of my segment.

yr a fucking goof, texts Frankie.

turn 2 food network rn, I text back.

Food Network happens to showcase a cooking competition where the final dish is dessert and they're tasked with making gelato.

jesus, Frankie texts.

im kidding im over it, I text back.

good for you

The next morning my phone is blowing up.

But even more thrilling is a notification that someone named P1L6R1M followed me overnight on IG. Pill six rim? What kind of Satan-worshipping video gamer is stalking my feed? It's Pilgrim. He's only posted three photos, and it looks like he's had his account for five months. They're all shots of him with a dozen or so other tough-looking jarheads doing their duty halfway across the world. Wearing fatigues. Greasing machinery. Pilgrim looks leaner, and he shaved that stupid chinstrap. He has a dumb grin on his dusty face, and he looks magnificent.

CHAPTER FIFTY-ONE

"MY NAME IS Annette . . . I'm calling from *Good Morning America*. I'm a producer, and I wanted to know if you'd like to come on the show."

"My name is Jerry, and I'm a producer with *The Ellen DeGeneres Show*."

"Hi, this is Loretta calling from *Jimmy Kimmel Live!*"

This is how I imagine it'll go. Wildest dreams. Shoot for the moon, because even if you miss, you'll be in the vastness of space, and every sci-fi spectacular has shown that right before you go cold, you'll be saved, last-second sucked into the air-lock room by randomly passing-by aliens.

Cut to me standing in the wings at *Ellen*, at *GMA*, at the *Today* show. Fifth show now, and I'm a media darling. Gotta strike while the iron's hot. I'm dancing with Ellen. Reenacting the piledriver with Al Roker in the fourth hour. Getting an on-air Skype session with the student I threw on *Jimmy Kimmel*.

Reality is that I get a few phone calls from local TV stations. Morning shows. A college public-access channel. Like I said, you can't predict what's going to play hot. That same week there's a bomb threat at a pop star's concert; kids are doing a new Hangman dance challenge; and a girl's hand fell off after she was slacklining, she cut it, it got infected, it got tossed, and now she's doing the media rounds, waving her stump, everyone calling her and her stump brave.

CHAPTER FIFTY-TWO

MOM'S GOT A surprise in store. Not for me, though. A splurge for her.

She's riding one of those super-expensive stationary bikes. The kind you have to tap into a mortgage to afford. She's even rocking the branded cleats. A touch screen the size of my laptop is strapped to the top, and Mom taps at different settings. I thought she was watching a replay, but turns out it's a livestreamed ride-along. A dreadlocked white woman in an exercise bra is talking into the microphone about radiating energy.

"How are you feeling, superstar?" Mom asks. She doesn't take her eyes away from the screen. She's pumping her fist intermittently. If this is the mom who was hidden away all those years due to penny-pinching single-parent survival, I want the cheap-ass back.

"I'm glad the kids made it out alive. Also, I'm lucky I didn't get into any trouble. Not going to lie, I was hoping something would come out of all of this." I take a seat on the sectional next to her, kick my legs up on the new ottoman.

"Didn't Terry mention he saw you?" Mom asks, grabs a water bottle from the bike cage and takes a big swig, all the while still pumping her legs vigorously. The water bottle is also branded.

"I don't think your neighbor waving me down and mentioning that he saw me on the evening news is exactly that brass ring."

"What do you think is next?" she asks. I can't tell if this is calculated or genuine offhanded small talk. I fiddle with the zipper of my hoodie, so smooth in its greeting teeth.

"I don't know. Can we talk another time, when you're not training for a triathlon?"

"Honey, you've got my full attention," she says. Her attention on the touch-screen instructor. Their heads bounce in rhythm.

"I don't know. Go back to school. Look for a new job."

"What about getting your own place?" Mom finally turns to me. Takes some breaths.

"Kicking me out already?"

"You're not the worst roommate I've ever had. But seriously, I want you to think about what's next. Not for me. For you. I'm not saying you have to pack your bags right away, but I want you to be looking ahead."

"I've got a few plans in the works. Know a buddy who knows a buddy. They're looking for line cooks and bar backs at this neighborhood place. Could probably get in pretty easy and start to save a few bucks."

"I believe in you, Ricky. But, Ricky, I want you to believe in me, too."

"What does that mean, Mom? Of course I do."

"Do you?" Her legs slow compared with the pace of her instructor. One of her cleats slips. She finds her footing again.

"Yes."

"Do you?"

"I said yes."

"I always felt like I did the best I could, but I did lie awake some nights thinking about whether or not I should bring a man into my life, into our lives. Maybe it would've made things easier. You feel that pressure when you're a young, single mother. Start to blame yourself." Her legs barely move. She's just keeping the machine on.

"Mom, I'm proud to be a Powell," I say, putting my hand on her shoulder. "I know you did your best."

"Love you, Ricky," she says, gives me a smile. "Now get your hand off my shoulder. You're throwing off my balance."

"Although I'm not going to go around screaming 'white power.'"

"White Powell," she says, picks up her pace. Rides to nowhere while listening to her crunchy instructor shout aspirational banter.

CHAPTER FIFTY-THREE

I GET A job at this greasy spoon off Seventy-Second called the Desert Eagle. Kitchen is industrial, but all we serve are burgers. All the patrons have names like Swamp and Darlene. I can't tell what vices Swamp got into early on in life. Meth, coke, drink. He looks sixty but says he's only thirty-eight. He coughs a lot, and half the time I have to make sure to give him good leeway because I think he's going to blow chunks. It always ends in dry heaves into his fist. And then, intent on fucking with me, he wants to shake hands after.

I come in and do dishes. Occasionally, I'll bar-back. Even less I'll flip burgers. Nights it gets busy, but there are downtimes. I'll read because that's a thing I continue to do. Every time Swamp catches me reading, he gives me an "Ooh la la!" Then calls me professor. But he's decent enough; slow nights he'll pull a travel-size Connect Four out of his bag and we'll go a few rounds.

I scrounge together a few hundred bucks. Eat peanut butter sandwiches for breakfast, lunch, and dinner. To switch it up, I'll eat tuna straight from the can. But only the packed-in-extra-virgin-olive-oil stuff.

I search for my own apartment. Can afford a roach hole in North O. But at least I'll be back on my feet.

I enroll back in school. Sign up at one of the community college satellites. I had a few credits from before I dropped. Not sure what avenue I want to pursue, maybe HVAC, culinary, there's even a greenhouse on campus where they teach classes about sustainability and beekeeping. My first class back, my English instructor, this Asian woman named Loan, tells us that we're going to learn how to pronounce her name. She has us discussing mental health, gender norms, homelessness. I ask her when are we going to learn about commas, and she laughs.

I didn't exactly cash in on media obligations. I wasn't waltzed onto *Ellen* to cash a big check. I'm no Walmart yodeler or pay-her-own-way middle school teacher. I physically assaulted a child—well, a teen. But things are good. Good as they've ever been. Mom and I speak twice a week on the phone and have lunch or dinner every other Wednesday. She's gotten into a soldering class at a different branch of the community college. I see Johnny America on occasion. He's still with Marfa. Have even run into Bojorquez in his Ford Fiesta.

And then one afternoon I'm feeling up fruit at No Frills. Trying to stay fit, but without a diet. Clean eating. A hot mom pushing her kid in a cart at five o'clock is closing in. I can tell she's hot based on aura alone. You know when someone attractive creeps into your periphery? I've definitely been wrong a time or two and thought it was a walking ten and it turned out to be a grandma in a poncho or a library drop-off box, but you can usually tell. I'm checking clementines for firmness when I feel a sharp pain in my heel. Chick clips me with her cart.

"The fuck?" I say, and look up at Frankie Rae Dillashaw. She's grown her hair back out. It's a little poufy, all natural. She's wearing denim overalls and a wide V-necked white T-shirt underneath. She looks a little stressed-mom unkempt. Still, she's so stunning that when we make eye contact, I feel like I lose all sense of myself and my skin sheds its water weight; I'm a shrink-wrapped me around a beating heart.

I stop breathing for a second. Two.

Then I see her kid sitting in the cart. Cute little girl with a frilly headband. She's wearing the kind of infant's formal shoes that don't actually get used. Bows. Clasps. She looks at me and grins; her just-peeking teeth give her a wild vibe.

"Adelaide, this is Ricky," Frankie says to us.

I instinctively reach out to shake her hand. She grabs my finger. We have a tiny shake. It feels official; baby business deal.

"How've you been, Frankie?" I ask.

"Great. We've actually got another on the way," she says, pats at her stomach. She's not showing yet.

"Congrats." I give her a shaky thumbs-up, like when your stepdad tells you to bunt in Little League but you don't know what the fuck a bunt is. Or so I've heard. Legit, I'm happy for her.

"Nice, Ricky."

"What?"

"That's so weak."

"I'm sorry. I really am happy for you."

"It's okay. How've you been? After that whole assaulting-a-child thing."

"Teenager. Assaulting a teenager."

She smiles at me. Adelaide farts. Giggles at her own wind.

"I'm doing all right. Got my own place. Mom is Mom."

"Tell her I said hi, okay?"

"You should call her, or stop by. She'd love that."

"You're right, I should," Frankie says, wipes Adelaide's dribbly chin with her hand.

"How are things going for you, though?" I try to do that thing where you roll an orb along your arm and catch it, but I drop the clementine and it rolls beneath a display. We both eye the spot where it disappeared, say nothing, and then turn toward each other.

"Great. Great. I'm going back to school. Finally saved enough to take ASL classes."

"Wow. That's awesome, Frankie. The only sign I remember is 'bullshit,'" I say, making one hand the horns and the other hand the turd flying out of the bull's ass. Adelaide looks at me and laughs.

"That would be the one you remember. Listen: I have to get going, gotta make dinner, but it was good seeing you, Ricky. Really." She looks over at my basket. "Good luck with your fruit salad. And store-bought sushi?"

"I haven't been able to eat at my favorite spot, so I have to settle."

"Why not?"

I lean in. Frankie gives me a quizzical look. "I have to tell you something that Adelaide can't hear."

We go for a real hug. For a split second, it echoes all the old ones. Familiar in a way that aches.

I whisper in Frankie's ear, "Mud flaps."

She laughs so hard she pulls back and snorts. Adelaide is even a little startled. Then Frankie leans back in. "NASCAR." We hug one more time. Adelaide waves bye. I wave bye back. I find the right firmness of fruit.

CHAPTER FIFTY-FOUR

AFTER THE MEDIA circus dies down, I get another phone call. Although it was less big-top circus than middle school carnival. I'm at the end of a work shift. Drenched in sweat, wiping my face clean with a dirty towel. Smelling like fry oil. Swamp is staring at me through the slot where we serve up orders. He's picking at his teeth with the edge of a Keno card. On the other end of the call is a Native American professor named Sandra Whitehorse. She says she reps a student-led Native organization through the state college and they're having a panel and they'd like a white person to be on it. Obviously, you won't be the focal point, but the university requires a certain demographic makeup in the conversation, she says.

First question: "Do you pay?"

"Yes, the university will give you a stipend of one hundred fifty dollars."

"I'm no scholar," I say.

"You leaving us, Ricky?" Swamp yells across the slot, like he can read my mind.

"We have scholars, we have community members. To be frank, we need a white guy. Makes the admins a little more comfortable. According to our students, you're a popular one." She says this to me point-blank. "You won't be talking all that much, but if the mic comes around to you, how do you feel about speaking in front of an audience?"

"I'm sorry, can you repeat that for me?"

"I said, 'Will you feel comfortable on the mic?'"

"I feel like it's my destiny, Wildhorse."

"Sandra is fine."

I'm behind the curtain again. Doing my breathing exercises. Four seconds, seven seconds, eight seconds. Just like Mom taught me. *I am a tender man, I am a tender man, I am a tender man.*

Cue the Maiden. I go running.

Acknowledgments

No prayer candle could do her justice. The patron saint of so many writers, my agent, Sarah Bowlin, who believed in this book sometimes even more than I did.

Thank you to Tracy Carns, who connected to the book on its Midwestern charms, and found it a lovely home at The Overlook Press.

Thanks to the whole team at The Overlook Press, including Eli Mock, Andrew Gibeley, Kimberly Lew, Mamie VanLangen, Jessica Wiener, and Lisa Silverman, among many, many others. I sincerely appreciate all your hard work in helping me get my book out into the world.

Speaking of The Overlook Press, special thanks to Charles Portis, who has been a hero of mine and was another reason I went with Overlook.

Thanks to mentors who helped me with guidance and good cheer when I needed it most. Thanks to Hugh Reilly, who was my biggest cheerleader when I didn't even know I wanted to be a writer. Teresa Lamsam, who was a great instructor at a time when I was waffling about even continuing with higher education. And Askold Melnyczuk, who talked to us less like students and more like peers and always treated our work with the utmost patience and respect.

Thank you to my Yale Writers' Workshop cohort, especially our fearless leader, Julie Buntin. Julie gave me so much confidence, especially at a time in my life when I needed it most. Julie has also gone above and beyond in making connections for me and I owe her so much.

Thank you to my Tin House "No Praise" folks, especially our ringleader, Catherine Lacey. Catherine has such a keen eye and a sharp mind. Her method involves not heaping on undue praise or harsh criticism, but immediately after my workshop, we met and she said, "I'm not supposed to say this, but this is great." Which is the best sign of a leader: knowing when to buck the rules.

Thanks to early readers like Jac Jemc and Paul Hansen and Mike Young who gave me the right push at the right time. Jac, especially, since she was the first one to read the whole thing and gave me stellar advice.

Thanks to others who said kind words and allowed me to slap them on the book, like Blake Butler, Gabe Habash, Kimberly King Parsons, and Sam Lipsyte. All of you inspire me so much, it's bonkers that you even considered reading my little ditty.

Thanks to friends far and wide who've always been in my corner, including Mike Schlesinger, Jordan Ateshzar, Shad Hovdenes, Michael McCauley, Anna Gebhardt, Lizzie Mytty, Paige Reitz, Brenton Gomez, Kenton Higgins III, Zach Schmieder, Daphne Calhoun, Anastasia Spracklin, Jeanette George, Nathan Ma, Matthew "Otus" Benak, Sean Pratt, Megan Siebe, Jean Kyoung Frazier, Ryan Ridge, Ashley Farmer, David Nutt, Gina Nutt, Ted Wheeler, Nicole Wheeler, Trey Moody, and a bunch of the folks I mentioned earlier whom I could mention again and again. Sweethearts and saints, all of you.

Lastly, thanks to my family, who are everything to me. Mom, Dad, Kevin, Annie, Mike and the kiddos: Enoch, Knox, Rock, and Mya. My stable. Forever and ever. Amen.